Man Without Face

Frances Itani

This book was written and published with the assistance of the Canada Council, the Ontario Arts Council and the Regional Municipality of Ottawa-Carleton.

"P'tit Village" was first published in *Queen's Quarterly* and *A Land, A People*. "An August Wind" originally appeared in *Fiddlehead* and *Contexts: Anthology Two*. "A Gift of Forty" first appeared in *Queen's Quarterly* and "Graveyard Shift" was originally published in the *University of Windsor Review*. Excerpts from "Flashcards" first appeared in *Canadian Forum* and *Nikkei Voice*. "Man without Face" originally appeared in *Prairie Schooner*. "The Granary" and "Earthman Pointint" were first published in *Canadian Fiction Magazine*. Blaine Harden's article on designer coffins in the *Washington Post* supplied background detail for "Earthman Pointing". The lyrics to "Susan MacGoozan" are from *Songs for Swingin' Housemothers* by permission of Fearon/Janus/Quercus.

ISBN 0 88750 952 5 (hardcover)
ISBN 0 88750 953 3 (softcover)

Cover art by Vittorio Fiorucci
Book design by Michael Macklem

Printed in Canada

PUBLISHED IN CANADA BY OBERON PRESS

For Teddy

P'tit Village

Été

It is whispered...Madame Lalonde...she asked the priest and
he said, "No," very firmly. What does it matter to him that
babies sleep in the same attic room, that children tumble over
bannisters, that they run through gangways pitching gravel
at old Hervé, the policeman, when he rides past on his bike?

It is whispered...Madame Lalonde...

"No."

"Again." Lips stretch thin and curl back over the news.

"Poor Madame. What will she do with them all? And he. He's no help to her, that good for nothing."

"He's tired, poor man. C'est ça."

At dusk the cross on the hill is set ablaze. You can see it for miles...from here, from there, from across the river. In daytime the children go to the top of the hill to look for blood, for miracles.

Madame Lalonde's is the last house on the dirt road that dwindles to grass and old tire tracks at the bottom of the hill. How that cross glows at night! The bulbs are replaced the very day they burn out. Or are peppered by the stones of hooligans. At night the cross carves its perpendiculars into Mme Lalonde's bedroom wall. Even from her bed she can see it. That cross.

Pitou lies on his side in the dusty road. It is dry, hot. Pitou has no energy. Get up, Pitou. Shoo. Leave him alone. What car ever comes here? Only the ice waggon and Pitou haslots of time to move before that old nag gets here. Monsieur, he walks to rue Principale and takes the grey rickety bus to work.

The children are playing in a field of golden-rod and blue thistles.

Am stram gram
Pic et pic et colégram
Bour et bour et ratatam
Am stram gram
Pic!

Amelie wants to go out, too. Not until the margarine is done. Knead the pellets till the colour bursts like shrapnel through the yielding bag. Pound it with your tiny fist, squeeze between the fingers. The colour spreads like a waxy orange a child might choose to paint the sun. Soon, the kneading is done; the margarine is uniform, harmless, yellow. Go out now, play, Amelie. Only till nine, mind.

The siren will shrill at nine. Ah yes, the curfew. From the top of the Town Hall the siren blows the children tidily off the streets. But it also injects excitement and fear into the hearts of the villagers. For if the siren wails and it is *not* nine o'clock you go to your back stoop to look for smoke. There is no fire truck here. Only the bucket brigade. That, and the siren, to summon the villagers.

Madame Lalonde has another mouth to feed. This one sleeps downstairs. Already, Madame and her husband have moved their own bed to the dining-room. No more space upstairs. If you creep to their window at night, you can see them undressing. In the light of the cross you can see them. Madame Lalonde is tired. Her breasts hang down, always being pulled and chewed and tugged. The baby sleeps in the carriage. Amédée they call him. A good name. A hungry devil, too, she says. M. Lalonde has a new job now. He wears a uniform. The children are proud; their father delivers Vachon cakes to the stores in the city. Now M. Lalonde revs the truck as he roars home, and Pitou has to pick himself up off the road.

Amelie is outside with her small brother, Jacques. Monsieur Poirot, the barber, has just cut Jacques' hair. Amelie has to go with her brother to make sure Poirot knows when to stop cutting. For Poirot keeps an extra bottle on his shelf. He also trades comics with the children when he's through.

Amelie and Jacques are returning home; it is 7:30 and they are leafing hungrily through the comics. The siren startles. Already? But it is not yet nine.

A little crowd clusters at the window of Mme Lalonde. Amelie and Jacques push their way to look through the limp net of curtain. From the back, Jacques' hair looks as if Poirot has turned a porridge bowl upside down.

Through the dining-room, through to the kitchen, they see their parents. Old Hervé is there, too. Hervé the policeman: it is his bike that lies on its side in the gravel. The younger children are spinning the back wheel, holding a cardboard to its spokes. Ra ta tah tat. There is something on the table...a baby, or a doll. A baby, yes, but this doesn't look like Amédée. This baby is blue and lies very still. Hervé bends over it, breathing into its mouth. Nothing. There is no cry. Nothing. Hervé breathes again and again. The child is fixed like a china ornament on the table. Mme Lalonde wrings her hands. It is no use. You can tell by looking at her face.

Make way! The priest has arrived. His shining black car thumps over the bumps in the road where grass has grown between old tire tracks. He stops in the puddle of gravel an inch from Hervé's bike. His black skirts swish as he walks to the door. "Leave the window, my children," he says to the sober faces in the crowd.

Poor Madame Lalonde. The cross has not even lit up yet, for the night.

When everyone has gone, she dresses Amédée's cold limbs in the gown in which he was baptized...he and all the others. It has been passed on all the way down from Joseph, the eldest. She stops for a moment beside the still bundle. The tears stream down her cheeks. She turns her head and spits on the scrubbed kitchen floor. Priest or no priest, there will be no other.

When the weather is warm, Hector, the chip man, emerges from his winter cocoon and plants his white cart squarely behind the horse in front of the Post Office. Tassé runs the Post Office from the closed-in verandah of his yellow house. The mail truck arrives from the city; Tassé sorts the letters into the shining silver boxes that line his verandah. The villagers come and go, up and down the steps, stopping to chat with Hector, slapping his old horse gently on the neck.

"Ah, Hector, back in business, you scoundrel. You've been

8

getting fat all winter...nothing to do but draw water. Come on, you dirty dog, give me some chips and make sure you fill up the bottom, too."

Behind the murky windows of his cart, Hector scoops thick fries, fresh from the splattering grease, into the cones of waxed brown paper. The children put their nickels on the ledge and hold their breath while Hector adds extra chips on top. As they walk away they cross their fingers, hoping the vinegar will stay in the bottom so they can suck it out when the last chip is gone.

When the mail traffic dwindles and the steps of Tassé's Post Office are empty again, Hector knows it is time for supper. He taps the loose reins against the horse's back, lets go, and the cart begins to wheeze up and down narrow side streets. The women run out to meet him, wiping hands on aprons as they hurry down the paths. They hold out their deep white crockery.

"Lots of mouths to feed, Hector, fill it to the brim." And dip their hands into the chips on the way back to their kitchens...after they've dipped into their apron pockets for the coins.

On Saturday afternoon the beerman comes. In the houses of the village, empties are stacked and ready. The beerman makes his rounds between two and four. Across the village you can hear the empties rattle and the children call, "Beerman! Beerman! La Bière!"

Mr. Smith, too, buys beer. Quincy and Marlene have gathered the empties and have put them by the porch door. They watch the gravel road to see who will come first: beerman? iceman? milkman? The iceman arrives; he carries the blocks of dripping ice in his steely picks all the way around the house, down the long gangway, through the back door. He bangs the block into the top of the icebox, pushes aside the small piece left over from yesterday, melted smooth as an ocean stone.

At the front, on the road, his horse jerks and halts, jerks and halts as the children cry, "Whoaaaa!" The children shinny up the back of the cart to the slippery boards and vie for slender ice chips to suck. Water drips through the waggon boards, leaving a chain of damp circles on the dusty road. The iceman returns and shoos the children away; he clucks to his horse.

If it is a hot day, Mr. Smith buys buttermilk from Borden's truck for his children. There is a picture of Elsie on the side of the truck—Elsie with the dancing eyes and curly horns. In August, Quincy and Marlene will be taken across the river to the Exhibition, and there they will see, year after year, the real *Elsie the Borden Cow* in her glittering stall.

At last, the beerman arrives. Mr. Smith pays his money and settles on the front step with his neighbour, Ti-Jean. There they will stay the entire afternoon, arguing, waving their quart bottles, deciding once and for all who *really* won in '59. No matter who comes out ahead, Mr. Smith reminds Quincy and Marlene inside, later: "It's ours by right of conquest!" His hand sweeps in an encompassing gesture out toward the land beyond the window. Quincy and Marlene are not so sure. They have had their own skirmishes and are outnumbered, after all. Dubious victors, they have rushed into their house and looked back out through the curtains at the taunting, conquered faces.

Everything around seems to be in a state of being dismissed or constantly damned. Yet nothing goes away—only, finally, and much later, Mr. Smith and his family.

Oh, how the children are bored this summer. They have cut bows and arrows from green saplings; they have fashioned whistles from reeds; they have played dead-man in the cove. They have scratched hopscotch into the dirt and have thrown cut glass onto the squares. What is there left to do? Visit Mon Oncle Piché on the verandah of his black wooden house!

Mon Oncle is everyone's uncle. He tilts in his wide rocker, all day, in shelter of the open verandah. He is too heavy to get up to walk around; it is enough effort just to get himself into his chair each morning. His head is almost as big as his belly with its layers and layers of hard fat. His hair is cropped short to his scalp, peppered with grey. His black pants, held by suspenders, fit straight up from thigh to chin. All day he sits on the verandah and eats bread and jam.

But Mon Oncle—how he loves the children!

"Viens citte, mon p'tit chou...come and talk to Mon Oncle."

The children tell him stories. He teases them; he knows more about them than their parents do. The children know that Mon Oncle can keep a secret. They make wishes and pop brown silky weeds against the back of his spotted hands. He tells them which leaves to smoke and where to find tender shoots of grass to suck. He knows which blossoms attract the whirr of hummingbirds' wings. He knows about crickets that sing and red-winged blackbirds in the swamp. He imitates the early morning *killdee-killdeer* until the call echoes back from the river.

The children wander off. Mon Oncle Piché sits alone and thinks of all the things he used to know. Then he turns to the propped-up tray beside his chair, and goes back to eating bread and jam.

In the warmth of evening, old Hervé, the policeman, sets out on his bike just as the nine o'clock siren wails to its highest pitch and drones to summer silence again.

"Off the streets. Off! Off the streets." He tries to wave his fist at the children but it is difficult to keep his balance on those dirt roads with only a single grip on the handlebar.

"Tabernac," he mutters as the children taunt, with one foot in their parents' yards, the other foot on the street. The leg of Hervé's trousers gets caught in the bicycle chain and he falls to one side, trying to extricate himself and look fierce at the same time. The silver badge is dull on his plaid work shirt. The children roll on the ground, puffing out their sides in fake laughter. The fender is bent and rickety as Hervé wobbles back toward rue Principale, the only street in the village that is paved.

But on Wednesdays, when the garbage truck comes round, the children do not laugh. Hervé's two big sons rattle the pails; they toss them back and forth with importance, with ease. They spit over the wheeze of truck and the stench of refuse.

"Maudit, don't get caught after the siren tonight. Our fadder, he will get you tonight."

Today, there will be a confession. In Quincy's and Marlene's backyard the children congregate beneath the overturned rowboat that rests on two shaky sawhorses.

No Protestant rite can match this. Marlene preens; she and Quincy will receive instruction from Pierrette and Hercules. Hercules will be priest.

The children kneel in the grass beneath the boat. Hercules' head manoeuvres the shadows somewhere above one of the wooden seats. His black eyes scrutinize the very souls of these young sinners.

"Do you have anything to confess?" Sternly.

"I laughed at Hervé when he fell off his bike."

"I swore at Pitou...and broke a plate."

"I wore shorts on Main Street. Against the priest's will."

"More? Robbery? Violence?"

"I had a bad thought in my heart," says Pierrette. Marlene is prepared for this. You have to confess all deeds committed and uncommitted. Those in your heart count for as much as the act.

"Any DIRTY thoughts?" Hercules asks this gleefully.

They shriek with laughter as he doles out the penance.

"Fifteen Hail Marys before supper." He makes the sign of the cross.

But the children are gone. Like the breeze they have scattered.

Jacques is sent to Chez Henri to buy peameal bacon. It is Thursday.

"We'll have bacon and eggs tonight," says Mme Lalonde. "Back to sardines tomorrow."

Jacques skulks to the store. He tosses tiny pebbles into the air, kicks a smooth round rock from square to square in the sidewalk. It must not touch a crack.

Jacques does not want to tell Henri to put anything on the bill—that pale lined pad, each page glaring accusation as Henri's wife presses down upon the carbon with soft pencil. At the end of the day the balance will be entered in the black ledger.

"Don't forget to tell your father to make a payment," she says.

Her plump breasts try to push sideways out of her flimsy cotton dress. Mme Henri goes to the hairdresser every week. Her hair is oiled and perfect, thousands of curls erupting from her plump head. Her skin, too, is oiled. Makeup the colour of brown eggshells lies in the creases of her neck.

When Jacques tells his father about the bill, Monsieur Lalonde growls, "What do those fatheads need my money for? They're robbing us blind, cal-ice."

Monsieur does not have to worry about the thick soft pages of the bill; it is not he, after all, who must face Mme Henri each day across the counter. No, Monsieur can afford to snub his nose at the store as he drives past each morning in his Vachon truck.

Summer's end. All week the river has been a mass of bobbing timber as the logs tumble and heave toward the Eddy mills. Half-mile downriver some of the logs pile in a defiant jam between the remnants of an old stone wall and a mossy island that is inaccessible because of rapids. Later, the men will work the rafts to free the main jams. They won't bother with the logs that drift to shore. In autumn, when the water rises, the strays will float out again.

The setting sun bursts golden beyond the trees. Water flings itself toward the roar of rapids. The sounds of night drift across the night air.

Automne

All fall the villagers have been fitting stovepipes, painting them with aluminum paint, banging out the soot, putting up the oil stoves, shaking down the ashes in the coal stoves. Scuttles stand ready. The coalman backs his truck into the yards, lowers his shute and sets the coal roaring into bins that have been sectioned off in corners of toolsheds and barns.

The last logs along shore have been pushed out by the children, or have floated away as the water has risen. Mon Oncle Piché sits on his verandah eating bread and jam, waiting for the children to come and sit beside him. He is sad because soon he will have to move his rocking-chair back to the kitchen by the stove, where he will sit all winter, eating, filling out the mass of his shapeless body.

School has started. The Protestants and Catholics are at it again. The boys can't wait to begin their snowball fights, and search the sky daily for signs of the first white flakes. For now, peashooters will do.

Mothers pull breeches and duffel coats from the attics. They trace around children's feet and cut cardboard soles to stuff into last year's galoshes, trying to make them last one more winter. They sew patchy fur collars onto coats, hiding claws, hoping to keep out the wind.

Hiver

A bluish-white covering muffles the village. Rue Principale quickly freezes and the children skate on the road at dusk. The rink boards are in place in the field and the barnboard shack with its potbelly heat is made ready. Music is pumped through a loudspeaker, which is attached to a pole at one end of the rink.

"Jaaallosseee Oh Donchoooo a toucha mee!"

The older girls skate round and round, flicking long dark hair, flashing eyes at young men who skate with an arm round the girls' waists. Legs are sleek and synchronized to the blaring music.

"Jaaallosseee..."

The orange school bus streaks into the village to collect the Protestants. Quincy and Marlene and another handful of English are driven to the one-room school miles away in the country. The Catholics have their own school in the village— a two-storey grey stone with black fire-escape clinging to the side. During the school term, the orange bus streaks in and out of the village, reminding the children that there are real differences to be considered. The older boys from both schools, the grade sevens, are appallingly monstrous and rowdy. In spring and fall they throw rocks; in winter they ambush with snowballs. The French on their way to school have to pass the English huddled at the bus-stop. Across the road there is a pond in a small open field, partly fenced in. The fence can easily be pushed down into the snow.

One day the boys are having their usual morning exchanges:

"I hope you freeze English."

"Pea soup and Johnny-cake
Make a Frenchman's belly ache."

"Mange la *marde*."

"Yellow belly."

"If you're so brave, walk on ice, English. We dare you."

The dare cannot be disregarded. The English swarm in conference and plump Protestant Quincy finds himself pushed out of the huddle amidst heroic cheers. He's accustomed to being teased about his weight, and goodnaturedly welcomes his first chance at bravado.

But Quincy does one better than walking on ice. He gets out into the middle of the pond and starts jumping up and down with his rolls of fat jiggling and the ice creaking and heaving. Marlene feels a nervous kind of hysteria rising in her. Everyone, French and English, stands giggling as the ice wobbles and cracks and bobs. And there is Quincy, not jumping now, but legs moving up and down on the ice in the slow pantomime that freezes time when something terrible is happening. Quincy's eyes are full of faraway fear; his head is just above the water line; ice chunks vibrate all around him. The boys are on the ice now, on their bellies, making a non-denominational chain to pull him out. They get him out, all right. He's even laughing. His red woollen toque sticks to his ears; its wetness seems to be steaming in the frosted air.

In winter, Hector's horse trots right out onto the frozen river. The crisp covering of snow holds a faint tinge of blue. Hector creates his own road with horse and sleigh—his old cart on runners. At the back the sleigh sags under two water barrels that fit against the floorboards.

As the weather gets colder, Hector chops away at the hole in the ice, for it is into the same place each day that he lowers his buckets. Even after a storm you can see the fine welts where the runners will slip in beneath the skin of snow. Hector's horse knows just where to go, just where to nudge the sleigh into the tracks. It jerks ahead, back, ahead, all the while Hector standing on that little step behind the barrels, reins in hand. The horse inches the sleigh to the edge and Hector lowers the bucket into the black current. Some days, before Hector is finished, the sun sets red and flat against the crusted river snow. The man curses, breathing rapidly. The horse stomps, snorting white clouds; frost clings to the hairs around its nostrils.

If it is dark by the time the barrels are filled, Hector hangs a lantern on the front of his sleigh as he starts his rounds. Door to door, he fills pails and jugs with drinking water. The yellow light bobs crazily across the night; the villagers hear the jingle of harness bells as the horse approaches. They sigh as they reach for their buckets and go out to intercept the bobbing yellow light.

"That Hector...it will be midnight before we get our water next time, you'll see."

In November, Mrs. Smith gives Quincy and Marlene the Sears catalogue so that each can choose one Christmas gift. There is an entire catalogue just for toys. It takes days and weeks to agonize over the choices. Skates? Meccano? So difficult, so lovely, to choose.

Quincy and Marlene have been saving since October. Every winter they trudge up and down the village streets showing *Sparkies Sprinkled Greeting Cards*. Every year their customers order the same box. Mme Laviolette invites them in; they remove galoshes and mittens and pull a chair to the kitchen table. Mme Laviolette is weary; she has been taking care of old Mr. Potts for years. He never gets better, but he never dies either. Mme Laviolette takes the poker and shakes down the ashes in the big stove. She brushes crumbs from the oilcloth on the table; she sits down and begins to leaf through the catalogue of novelties and cards. When she is finished, she examines the sample boxes. Cats leap at one another from dark corners. Quincy and Marlene hold their breath. Mme Laviolette pushes back her chair; she stands wearily and orders *Sparkies Economy Box* of 36 assorted greetings. No matter what time it is when Quincy and Marlene arrive, it is always dark when they leave. No-one has ever ordered novelties but almost everyone needs a box of cards. For every box they sell they get a dime.

On the second Saturday in December, Quincy and Marlene go shopping in the city. Mrs. Smith pins purses into pockets, gives last minute warnings, watches through the frontroom window as they cross the field to the bus-stop.

The bus shakes and rattles along the old gravel road until the children think their teeth will fall out. They are deposited at the end of the line in front of E.B. Eddy where they must take a streetcar across the river: past the mill, past the falls, past the greasy spoons, into the centre of the city.

The first stop is Woolworths, for lunch. They pace the food counter as carols blare and startle overhead. They remove one dollar and twenty-nine cents from each purse and scrutinize pictures of club sandwiches, french fries, hot fudge sundaes. When at last they are able to find stools side by side, they hoist themselves up and order two Christmas specials with the works: turkey, cranberries, one scoop of mashed potato, one of pale turnip, a spoonful of dressing, a scattering of peas. For dessert, a banana split. As they eat, they watch lifts shoot up and down; they hear voices from the bowels of kitchens below. Waitresses pounce upon stainless containers of chicken salad; up come butter and chocolate syrup in silver bowls. Quincy and Marlene twirl gently on their stools, sifting and storing every sight and sound.

When the spirit of Woolworths is inside their bellies, they swivel down and head for the displays of powder puffs, ashtrays, pickle dishes, for it is here that they will purchase their gifts.

Christmas Eve, Mr. and Mrs. Smith tell Quincy and Marlene they may stay up for Midnight Carol Service. They have to take the eleven o'clock bus to town because the Protestant Church is fifteen miles from the village. They arrive early and wait in the church basement while members of the choir dress in flowing robes and four-cornered hats. The children do not like to hear the choir talking of ordinary matters. They prefer to see them dressed, whole, gowned and singing loftily like angels. When the first strains of the organ are heard, the members of the choir throw out their chests and roll their eyes to the sky.

Home again, the Smiths go next door to visit Ti-Jean and his family who have returned from Mass. Madame has baked tourtières and pigs-in-blankets, neat brown bits of pork curled inside crisp pastry. Flasks and glasses crowd the edge of the kitchen table. Everyone sings:

D'où viens-tu bergère
D'où viens-tu?

Je viens de l'étable
De m'y promener
J'ai vu un miracle
Ce soir arrivé

Soon, everyone hushes, for Madame and her daughter are going to sing *Minuit Chretien* in their silver-toned soprano voices.

The Smiths return home, crunching over moonlit snow. The swamp at the edge of the field has frozen and cat-tails are trapped along the surface ice. Peace sifts down over the village.

The last event of winter is *Carnaval*. There will be dog races, songs, snow sculptures, skating prizes at the rink. Everyone must wear a costume. The mayor and the priest will judge. Pierrette and Hercules will dress up, as will Quincy and Marlene, Amelie and Jacques. Any child old enough to wear skates is included, even the ones who have to crawl on hands and knees across the fields to get there.

Pierrette's mother airs out her husband's longjohns, gets out the ragbag, begins to sew. Pierrette will be a rabbit; her trapdoor in the rear hangs down to her knees; white fluff is plastered to her leggings underneath to make a fuzzy tail.

Quincy will be Aunt Jemima; his friends call him Tante Jemeem. For a night and a day, two of the large brass curtain-rings will come down from the window to adorn Quincy's vainglorious ears. Mrs. Smith smears cold cream on his cheeks and darkens his skin with ox-blood shoe polish. A bolster from the armchair is stuffed inside his jacket. On top of all, a colourful blouse Aunt Minn has donated for the occasion, and a long woollen skirt that stretches to the ankles of his black skates. The final touch—a plaid bandanna from Grandma Smith's old trunk.

Everyone comes to *Carnaval*. Hervé, the policeman, and Poirot, the barber, dress up as a horse; someone plays crack-the whip with their tail. A thin Père Noël arrives, even though it is February. He has leftover cinnamon-tasting hard candies to give away.

All the little ones receive a prize. The older children are judged. The priest favours a tramp. The mayor? He likes the St. Bernard with the keg around its neck. They compromise...both St. Bernard *and* the tramp are awarded 50 cents.

The priest goes back to the church, his skirts billowing around hidden legs. Everyone comes out on the ice to sing. The men swell their chests:

Chevaliers de la table ronde
Allons voir si le vin est bon

Allons voir oui, oui, oui
Allons voir non, non, non
Allons voir si le vin est bo-o-on

Bottles are pulled from pockets; the keg is borrowed from the St. Bernard, filled and passed around. The villagers sing and sing...and finally, everyone goes home. Monsieur Poirot and Mr. Smith walk together, arms around shoulders:

Prendre un p'tit coup
C'est agréable
Prendre un p'tit coup
C'est doux!
Prendre un gros coup

Ca rend l'esprit malade
Prendre un p'tit coup
C'est agréable

Prendre un p'tit coup
C'est d - o - u - x !

Printemps

With spring come the storms. The villagers keep flasks of holy water handy on the shelf. Waves whip across the widest part of the river, lashing shore. Lightning splits the sky and the holy water is grabbed from the shelf, sprinkled outside and in, a little here, a little there. But not everyone is blessed. The Fournier's house goes up in flames, nothing saved but the old wringer washer and two kitchen chairs.

Storm after storm...the holy water dwindles. Run to the church, mon fils; run, ask the priest for another bottle. Light the candles inside; say your prayers; hold your breath; listen for the siren. The tall wooden houses shudder and moan in the wind.

The sun shines. Flowers bloom. In the damp cedar woods grow trilliums, dogtooth violets, lady's slipper, *petit prêcheurs.* Open fields are swollen with tough stalks of blue chicory and snapdragons that the children call butter-and-eggs.

Madame Lalonde tells the children: "No swimming until the first day of June." They whimper and coax and whimper some more but she will not budge. It is all a façade, really; early in May each year, Amelie and Jacques sneak away from the hill, down along the road until they come to the river. Here they slide down shale and loose rock until they are at the swollen bank. The water is crystal, numbing cold. They cross their hearts and spit, swear never to tell; then, off with the shoes and stockings. Spring water laps between the toes. Amelie holds her skirt above her knees so that no dampness will show around the hem. Goosebumps erupt on her legs and skin. Her toes cramp with pain; her ankles are white with cold. Amelie and Jacques wade back to shore. Dry their feet in the breeze, on with shoes and socks, walk with a light step, run, *race* the last stretch that turns to gravel in front of their home.

Even if it is 90 degrees on the thirty-first of May, Mme Lalonde says, No, they must wait. No swimming until the first of June.

The children scamper about in their underpants, giggling and tripping one another. They form a line on either side of her as they solemnly cross the field. Mme Lalonde swishes along in thick skirts; she holds high a mound of worn towelling.

The neighbours look out the windows and watch the march. "June the first," they sigh. "There goes Madame with her brood to deposit the winter lice on the riverbottom."

One by one Madame takes each little one out to the current, wading as deep as the child's knees. Dips the body, soaks the thick brown head. Together they watch white suds swirl around the legs, bubble and streak out on quick waves toward the mainflow. The head dips again, once, twice. The hair squeaks, smooth, no tangles. The way it would be if washed in the rain barrel.

Along the riverbank white birches toss gently their slender bandaged limbs.

Saint-Jean Baptiste Day at last! Even the dogs will be fancy, wearing crimped paper collars. The children have woven gay patterns of pink and white crêpe through the spokes of their bikes. The younger ones hold high their windmills on sticks and run through the wind. The big bonfire will be set beneath the cross, in the field beside Mme Lalonde's. All week the villagers have been gathering sticks, dead trees, an occasional pilfered log from the bank of the river.

The priest drives a big truck, stopping before each house in the village. The older boys help with the collection and chant,

"Food for the poor! Food for the poor!" Everyone gives something, even the poor. A tall young man stands in the doorway rattling the priest's money box while the woman of the house makes a choice from her pantry. A can of peas will do. The priest supervises from the cab of the truck; the big boys climb back, hanging on to the high boards, making important noises as they rumble through the streets.

Just before dark, the procession begins. It winds its way like a tattered dragon around the dirt roads and down rue Principale. There is one float and this is covered with tissue flowers.

The children spin and whirr their bikes as they ride first beside the float, then beyond, turning again to rejoin the parade. The dogs become silly and nip daringly at ankles and fleshy limbs. There are three old cars in the procession, and one big truck. The older boys are up there again, making the same important noises. The priest joins, sleek in his new black car. When the last of the stragglers has reached Mme Lalonde's field, everyone fans out in a circle around the heap of wood and scrub.

Will the timing be precise? The air hangs heavy. All is still. The cross on the hill leaps into brilliance. Yes!

The priest prepares a torch and lights dried branches and kindling. "Ahhhh!" The crowd tilts back. Soon the sky roars with fire. Flat rocks beneath the wood snap and crack in the heat; hot stone splinters across the night. The celebration becomes noisy and joyous. There is much singing. Each of the children receives a little bag of hard candy. Some of the candies are stuck together—still left over from last year's Christmas party and from *Carnaval*.

Third week of June, the orange bus drives away for the last time. The English shove remnants of their school year out the bus windows; the French scatter their scribblers into ditches along both sides of the road.

No more pencils
No more books
No more teachers' dirty looks

The children, French, English, Protestant, Catholic, bury their differences for the summer. Together they explore the swamp in sunlight, picking marsh marigolds brighter than buttercups. They sneak up on frogs that have eyes like peeled grapes, peering over cloven lily pads; they lie in wait for hours, scooping unsuspecting tadpoles into jam-jars for backyard aquariums. When they are bored, the boys chase the girls, threatening with garter snakes that twirl from their wrists. The girls turn their backs, bend, expose the insult of white cotton bloomers.

Halfway through summer, construction crews arrive to work on the dirt road; they begin to carve out a highway. Rock is blasted into the air, settles in mounds, cracked and splintered.

"There goes the Canadian Shield," says M. Lalonde. "Sky high! Fhooomph!"

At the end of summer, the logs will travel the *real* highway, the river. Brimful of bobbing timber, edge to edge, every log stamped with company initials. Not that this keeps the villagers from pulling in the strays, sawing them into equal lengths, chopping them up for firewood.

At nine, the siren wails. Hervé climbs on his bike. The sun sets. A remote hand pulls a switch. On top of the hill the cross blazes once more.

Madame Lalonde sighs. "That cross!"

The Granary

Early September, Magda and Travers book themselves into a
guest cottage in the central portion of The Lizard. The cottage
is an old stone granary, made over, with comfortable furniture
and real antiques. The farmhouse is across a dusty court where
geese pick about much of the day, or sit watchful under open
sheds. The main entrance of the farm is around the other side. A
dirt lane, hidden from the passing road, leads to the granary a
back way, through fields of parting corn. Magda and Travers
can drive through the corn without being seen from the paved
road or the farm and for Magda, this is the attractive feature of

25

the place. She doesn't have to look at anyone and no-one has to look at her; she's in enough of a glass bowl on the Berta Louise. About this time every year she believes that if she doesn't get away, she'll take a grand and final leap from the first-class deck.

"Out of all eyes," Travers says, teasing her about her annual but necessary reclusion. But he knows when to stop; they've worked side-by-side for eleven years, ever since she applied to become ship's nurse. He's been on the Berta Louise longer but he hasn't actually said how much longer and she leaves it at that. She,too, knows enough to pull back before the prying questions.

Magda and Travers do not sleep together; they're much too intimate for that. They began to take holidays together after they'd known each other only one year, and now here is Travers turning 50. The years spin off like sun's rays over the sea. Magda stows in her foreground memory: *Remember to buy a cake; half a century deserves a celebration.* Champagne, too, not expensive but not cheap. Fifty is a birthday she'll have herself, in a year and four months, during the shrunken colourless days of January. If she'd been born during a hot florid summer, who knows, her life might have been entirely different.

Not one to daydream, she stops herself right there. She's had her failed marriage; Travers has had his.

Travers tells people, when they ask, that he's in entertainment. What this means is that he hires magicians, singers, dancers, what he privately calls his washed-up celebrities. The Berta Louise pays the entertainers a stipend and free passage from Montreal to Le Havre, providing they perform. Sometimes, Travers hires writers or playwrights too broke to pay their own passage; he can get them for much less. What they must do in return is a talk or a reading in the Beaver Room, two afternoons during the crossing. Intemperance sometimes becomes a problem with his celebrities but Travers is an old hand; he rings Magda in the Infirmary and sends the recalcitrants to her. The two have perfected a remedy over the

26

years on board, the first part of which is captivity. Once Magda has her patients in the Infirmary, she doesn't let them go. The second part is this: she sits the inebriated person on a hard-backed wooden chair and has him or her drink lukewarm water, glasses, jugs, gallons of it. Though it makes them pee a lot, it sobers them up. Foolproof. Absolutely foolproof.

There are two rooms in the granary: a large room with a stone divider between kitchen and living-room, and one medium-sized bedroom. There's a pull-out couch in the living-room and when this is untangled and unfolded—cushions removed, cushions replaced—it becomes a floor-bed. Travers is stretched out on this, though it's three in the afternoon. Magda has said she'll cook and is on the other side of the divider putting together, treat of treats, a beef stew. The menu on the Berta Louise, even for crew, is much too good to include stew, so this is one of the indulgences of their first 48 hours ashore.

"You may be the one turning 50," Magda says, "but let me tell you what's been happening to me." She jabs at the cubes of floured beef, which are sizzling in salt and pepper, cloves and fat. She thinks she'll die of pleasure inhaling the scent. "Every time I meet a child, now, I find myself searching its face for the old person it's going to become."

"I wouldn't worry about *that*."

"I'm not. What worries me is that I can't keep myself from doing it. All my life I've done just the opposite, watched old faces for a hint of the child they used to be. Surely, that's significant. Now you, for instance. You're not old but your boy-face is inside your adult face. Smack in the centre like a saucer within a plate. It's like finding a thin face within a fat one...you're not the least bit fat, don't get me wrong."

"Thanks, just bleeding thanks."

"I've begun to practise opposites, don't you see?"

"What about Teeny-bird? What did you see in her face?"

"Teeny's a nest of dry twigs, the skeleton's already coming through. Jesus God, I didn't think she'd make it off the gangplank. Weren't you afraid she'd collapse into a heap of sticks? I had her down for a heat lamp on her shoulder and my fingers nearly went through to the other side of her."

Teeny had been a recent passenger whose age could not be known; she was old and miniature, just over four feet and covered herself with pieces of crocheted cotton, which made her look like a moving tea-cosy. Even on her head she wore a two-inch-high mauve cover that looked like Nehru's hat.

"Teeny's hard to guess. Nobody could see the child in that. Her face has almost disappeared." Magda figures Teeny is the oldest person she's ever met.

"But she had everyone hopping, didn't she."

"Money," Magda says firmly, giving the stew a poke. "You couldn't see the child in her but you could see the money."

"Speaking of...shall we make the kitty?" Expenses are split carefully down the middle.

Magda pours in a can of tomatoes and breaks them up with a wooden spoon she's found in a crock.

"You go ahead. Ten pounds for a start? Fifteen? I'll add mine when I finish here."

"How about fifteen? We'll want a little something..."

Their drinking tastes are the same, a bottle of wine, good Scotch, there's never any fuss. Magda thinks of the champagne she'll buy. Not out of the kitty.

"Shall we have the stew tonight, Magda? Or tomorrow? To age or not to age. If it's for tonight I'll go out now, for the wine. Might as well have a dollop for the pot."

"We'll have it tonight, thank you. It can simmer all afternoon. If you'll hold your horses, I'll come with you to get the wine."

She thinks of the passengers who overeat on the Berta Louise. Indigestion is the most common complaint to reach the Infirmary. She and Gilbert—he's Medicine and Surgery in one, the fourth doctor she's worked with in eleven years—dispense more antacids, more gas pills. It's the huge and stale joke of their existence. She thinks that one day she'll make up

28

a song about flatus and belt it out from Travers' platform above the dance floor. To the overfed, overstuffed, overweight passengers with their bowels rumbling and ruminating. That, and sea-sickness. The least swell of the ocean and someone can be counted on to toss their biscuits, usually at the top or bottom of a carpeted stairway. She's glad she isn't the one who has to clean it up.

Not that she and Gilbert don't deal with conditions more serious. Timmy, the child who'd aspirated the peanut. The emergency tracheotomy they'd performed. She broke out in goosebumps just thinking about it. Holding the child's limp body against the stretcher, Gilbert's clean quick stroke with the scalpel, the tiny curved tube sliding in swiftly. Miraculously, they got the peanut out. They had so little time. The child's colour cleared almost immediately but, later, red pinpoints appeared in the whites of his eyes and on his cheeks. The rupture of all those tiny blood vessels from the pressure. The ship was close to the coast of Ireland, thank Jesus God, and they got him and his family off and transferred him to hospital.

She remembers the sleepy passengers who'd stayed up all night to cheer Ireland, their first glimpse of land in five days. The air was cold and they were wrapped in orange blankets pinched from the deckchairs; they looked like penguins stumping and gliding about. A drunken hurrah had gone up at the sight of land; more than a little champagne was spilled that night. But a hush dispersed their silliness when the coastguard was seen approaching and the transfer took place. She and Gilbert did not have to disembark; a doctor had come from shore to accompany the child. Oh, they'd felt good over that one, grim as it was.

As if reading her mind, Travers says, "Did you ever hear anything of the boy who choked on the peanut?"

"Timmy," she says quickly. "His mother sent a card. We got it two months later, Gilbert and I. He was right as rain. He wanted to know did the sparrow live."

"The sparrow. I'd nearly forgotten. Do you remember how

he'd fill the saucer for it?"

"I remember."

But she hadn't thought of it in a good while. The pathetic bird had drifted off course, flown out too far. It had materialized out of the mist and landed on deck halfway across the North Atlantic. The poor thing was shivering and starving and the crew adopted it. It hopped about on deck and they set up a shoebox shelter, away from the passengers. Timmy used to come and pour water in its saucer and squat quietly beside it and talk softly, the bird perking up at the child's voice. The bird had survived though it ended up on the wrong continent.

Magda pokes furiously at an onion and tries to keep it from rising to the surface.

"Tintagel tomorrow?" Travers says. "It's not all that far, a day-trip, I think."

"Lots of climbing, I'll bet."

"Can't be that bad. Wear your old clompers. We'll take another pair in the car so you can change for tea."

"And you'll wear your Elvis boots." It's a joke between them that he looks like an ageing Elvis. He's getting round in the middle and thin on top though he has thick sideburns that he brushes back. But his eyes, they're a blue of the palest wash. Magda thinks they look as if someone has given them a good rinse.

"King Arthur's birthplace, Magda. He's an elusive man. They've made a fool of him all the way down the line. He was real for God's sake but he's been made into a cardboard figure, a backdrop for all the other knights. He sits at the Round Table, receiving, dispatching. The truth is...the truth is...there was a time when he slew 960 of his enemy in a single attack."

She looks back, over the divider.

He shrugs. "I'm only telling you what history says."

"I wouldn't know an Angle from a shingle, Travers."

Sometimes she becomes impatient with him even though he knows interesting things. And he knows more than he lets on. It's a condition of their friendship that neither pries nor spies but there is a period during each of their holidays, for instance, when he disappears. He stays away two nights and returns like the prodigal, contrite and weary. Rings under his eyes and lids swollen nearly shut. S-E-X she thinks, each time, but she's not certain whether it's with man or woman.

She herself hasn't had S-E-X with anyone since she slept with that woman's husband on the Berta Louise. He'd come to her room at night and tapped at the door, bold enough to invade the crew's quarters, bold enough to have learned the location of her cabin. And she, Magda, had let him in. She'd seen him around, he seemed to be everywhere: in the pool, at the film, lined up at morning sick-call for antacids, in the ballroom dancing with slim-hipped sylphs after Travers' floor show was over. She never even knew his name, Jesus God forgive her.

His wife had come to her, weeping, two days earlier, in a fit of depression. Wanting to talk that was all. Magda was used to any sort of problem banging at the Infirmary door. The marriage was over, the woman said so. But he criticized her for the way she talked in the Card-Room, for jokes she told in the Dining-Room. "He says it's all bullshit," she sobbed. "But what he has to say is bullshit, too. And my bullshit is just as funny as his." She and Magda had looked at each other then, and started to laugh, shaking and bent over, great belly laughs hiccuping out of them.

Perhaps the woman had told him she'd discussed their private lives. But Magda had heard worse than that. She'd listened to tales of woe; she'd watched bodies break down in shameful ways; she was not the least surprised at the sudden turns marriages would take. She didn't know the game these two were playing and she didn't care. To her it was all the same, it was called Life. But the walls of her cabin had rocked that night. The colour rises to her cheeks, thinking about it, and she keeps her back to the divider so Travers won't see.

A rooster hops up the stone steps at the kitchen door and

with an awkward flap of wings that can be heard inside, perches on the iron railing and peers in. At the same moment the geese pick themselves up out of the dirt and grudgingly cross the yard. Magda watches them settle in a grumble of honks, as if their relocation has been an aggravating necessity.

She thinks of Timmy, squatting beside the sparrow with his saucer of water. She thinks...she thinks...she does not allow herself to think. She stirs the stew, hitting the sides of the pot with the wooden spoon.

There he is before her, her five-year old Thom, playing in the farmyard on their small acreage in Canada. Twenty-one years ago; he has been allowed to call one gosling his own. The gosling runs after him, roly-poly with down. The child leads the way, zigzagging through the dirt. Laughter spills out of him like beads without a rattle; laughter for its own sake, free of care, free of necessity.

She has just come home from her day-shift at the hospital; she is still in uniform and stands in the kitchen, turned toward the window. Thom bends at the waist and then, squats beside his pet. He's in brown short pants, blue socks and sneakers; he's wearing a white T-shirt, which his father has given him and which has the words *Gaggle-Gaggle* printed across the front. His father tickles him when he wears that shirt.

Thom wraps his fingers around the beak of the gosling; his small hand makes an enclosing fist. The pet instinctively tugs its head back and forth. Even though the child holds its beak gently and playfully, the gosling cannot free itself. It plants its feet in the dirt and tries to pull backwards. At this, Thom reaches into his pants pocket and pulls out a fistful of something Magda cannot see but knows to be cracked corn. He lies on his back and sprinkles the corn over his chest. He lifts the gosling and it pokes and tickles as it eats the corn. The child giggles and giggles.

Gaggle-Gaggle.

She gets up to leave the room when the nurses enter to suction the white froth that bubbles up from an unending well inside his tiny chest. This time, she is not in uniform; she is a visitor on the Intensive Care Ward. She has just prayed that Thom will not live another night because he has been in coma for eight days and his pupils have dilated so widely the colour of his eyes can no longer be seen. He is what is called brain-dead though the nurses and doctors, all of them her friends, are careful not to say this in front of her. She was not with him when the speeding car struck as he skipped along the edge of the dirt road. Even though his father was the one who had to witness the fact of it with unbelieving eyes, she is the one who goes over and over every detail in her mind, a horror that she cannot keep from unfurling.

Travers' arm is around her. He's put the lid on the simmering stew though she doesn't remember him doing this.

He lifts a towel from the back of a chair and dabs at her eyes. "You went all silent after the rooster jumped up. I was blathering away, all that stuff about King Arthur. I didn't know you were upset."

But they don't pry.

"Timmy," she says. For he doesn't know about Thom.

"Is that it?" He hugs her awkwardly. "You saved him, it was a wonderful thing you and Gilbert did. You were able to save the life of a child."

She feigns a gentle push against him but at the same time moves in such a way that she gathers together all of her shifting bones. She gives an involuntary shudder, the way someone does after a long cry when there are no more sobs and no more tears to come. It rocks her from some place deep inside herself that she cannot still. She watches Travers' face contort and she wills her body to obey.

They head for town by the dirt lane, driving through the parting corn. From the driver's seat she looks over at Travers.

"So. You're 50," she says, thinking of the champagne. "Fifty deserves a celebration."

33

In the Yellow House

The fifth night in the yellow house Eleanor heard scratchings. She was at the kitchen table, reading. Cass had been tucked in since nine; Robert had fallen asleep in bed with his glasses on and his neck crooked at an angle that could only have been comfortable on the *Guernica* canvas. Eleanor went into the front bedroom—the one from which the sea could be both seen and heard—and touched him on the shoulder.

"Robert, I think there are rats under the sink. Or in the walls. Or behind the cupboards—maybe even *in* the cupboards. I'm afraid to open the doors in case some creature jumps out at me."

Robert removed his glasses and rubbed the back of his neck. Eleanor stood at the side of the bed, waiting.

"It's mice, Eleanor. For God's sake, there are always mice in these old farm places. Mice make a lot of racket."

"They were never here before."

"Maybe winter's coming early this year. They know things we don't."

It was easy for him to say; she was the one who sat up every night, reading. Eleanor went back to the kitchen but kept the broom at hand. She tightened her black shawl over her shoulders.

Chewing. It was a steady gnawing and chewing. She thumped the broom handle against the wall. The noise stopped abruptly but began again as soon as she started to read. She imagined a mouse with a sheaf of drywall in its teeth. She stamped her feet. All quiet. Turned a page. Steady confident chewing, then. She gave up. Resigned herself to another week in the company of rodents that would bore patterns in the walls around her.

Robert was right. It was the end of summer. The field mice must be needing winter places. The combines roaring up and down the fields in clouds of dust and chaff had dislodged many creatures, not only mice. Parker had told her that. Parker, who owned the land and this house though he himself lived across the field on the other side of Government Road. This afternoon he'd bent over in the field and picked up a dead mouse by the tail, as if there were dead mice everywhere you went to place a foot. He'd tossed it away, over the fence. To show her. He'd laughed, but not meanly.

What Parker and Robert and probably even eight-year-old Cass didn't question was that the company of mice was an ordinary event in the life of a farmhouse that had been dragged to the edge of a field of barley but which had, at its front windows, a cliff and an endless marvellous stretch of sea. That was the trade-off. Eleanor looked at her page and tried to concentrate. She gave up, turned off the light and stared out the window. She tried to imagine. She tried to imagine sea. What she saw was blackness, a blackness more unsettling than the even louder crunching around her.

Everything was wrong. In the morning she and Robert irritated each other, even knowing the stakes. Cassie, not knowing, was caught between. Eleanor made efforts to stay out of Robert's way. He took Cass for a walk on the beach. He was going to fly home at the end of the week; she and Cass would drive back, after Labour Day. "Someone has to get the bacon," Robert had said. This was while they were still at home, making plans. Eleanor reeled as if she'd been slapped. "Eleanor, it was a joke..." But she'd turned away, had gone into the bedroom and cried without noise, watching her face in the mirror. He hadn't meant it but it had slipped out of some brooding place of his own. Some place where he believed she wasn't doing her share?

She was the one, they both knew, who had to decide. And Eleanor knew that a woman who has conceived is a woman who has been outfitted with blinders; there was only one direction: ahead, ahead, ahead. A horizontal law of gravity: what goes in must come out. Whether she wanted a baby or not, whether she liked the way her body had deceived her or not, her only choice now, was over *what* would come out of her—a living baby or an early mass of cells. No, not cells; she forced herself to say it—dead baby. Cells were multiplying at this very moment while she thought and breathed and stretched her body in the sun, on this wooden verandah.

Cassie came running up the steps and dumped a bucket of shells at Eleanor's feet. "Dad's taking me to town," she said. "We're going to get ice cream. And come back and watch TV."

Robert came up behind Cass and shrugged. He and Eleanor hated TV. "It's Cassie's holiday," he said, as if this were news.

Eleanor was thinking of the mice. Maybe the sound from the television would blast them out of the walls, back to the fields. Maybe, but not likely. They'd taken up lodgings. For the winter. Last fall, one of the women at the Refugee Centre where Eleanor worked had related a story about her home being "troubled" by mice. The woman—her name was Fiona—had set traps in the basement and kept one contaminated work glove near the traps. A designated glove, to deal with corpses. The glove had been burned after the "trouble" had been cleared up.

It was Fiona who'd commented one day, while the women at the Centre were discussing abortion: "My great-grandma was a midwife—in the country. The women of the district came to her when they didn't want to go through with their pregnancies. She'd say to them: 'If you're meant to lose it, you'll lose it on a hiccup; it you're meant to have it, you won't budge it with a stick of dynamite.'

"Have you ever heard of a saying like that?" Fiona said. "I still don't know if she really did abortions."

All of this was before Eleanor had missed her period. Before the test. She was, she calculated again, four and a half weeks, possibly five. But she remembered the "trouble," the glove, Fiona's great-grandma. Fiona's great-grandma had also known about skirlie and hot mustard baths and doses of quinine. But you'd only lose it if you were meant to.

Fiona was safely past middle-age. Or not. Eleanor had thought *she* was safe. With Cass, she'd stayed home because she wanted to, until Cass was in school. She and Robert had agreed—one child. When she looked at Robert, now, she wanted to hit, to strike him.

As soon as Robert and Cass drove off, Eleanor left the house and made her way down through the dune paths. She dropped onto the beach from a ledge three feet above the sand. Wind and salt had eroded the face of the sandstone cliff, which looked as if it were releasing a hidden city, one that was emerging slowly, from within. She faced east, then west, trying to decide. She chose east and headed toward a tall rock that stood in the water offshore like a hoodoo. She needed space. She had come here for space but was crowded with Robert here. She knew she could not decide until he left at the end of the week. She should have come alone or just with Cass, not having the luxury of time.

The sea was blue green, and silent. She could see the high-tide line far up on the beach. In the night, while they were sleeping—she remembered this from other summers, too—the sea crept in where it never came by day, except in storms. It was a mystery, this creeping up. She always wanted to get out of bed in the middle of the night and stalk it. Sneak round from the higher cliffs and see how far the waves washed in.

Every evening this week, she'd sat at the kitchen window while there was still light in the sky and wondered what it was that held the sea in place. Even though the old house was high on a cliff, she imagined the sea to be higher. Five days, now, she'd been staring at it, watching it bulge against the horizon. Holding under the surface what another part of her knew was there. An energy, a force that might be released at a whim.

She walked farther than she'd intended, the hoodoo always in sight. She could see cormorants hovering, settling on top. She made that her destination though she knew by the distance already covered that it was more than three miles and she'd be facing a long walk back.

As she neared the rock the sea became dark, almost black. The hoodoo was an island of its own about 50 feet offshore, populated only by cormorants. The largest of these seemed too heavy to fly; the water between the cliffs and the hoodoo too deep to wade through. She looked up along the clifftops at grass and clover and wild strawberry, grown to the edge. Several plants hung upside down where the red clay had crumbled above the root structure. Jagged steps had been hewn into the wall of the red cliff. She knew there was a farm just over the rise—one of Parker's neighbours—but from the beach the farm was out of sight. She climbed the steps, holding on to some of the larger jutting rocks above her.

At the top she pulled herself over to the grass, satisfied. To the west along flat cliff-tops she could see the yellow house on a point overlooking the sea. It seemed tiny in the distance. She squinted, trying to decide if the car were back. Probably not. From the other direction, from the farmhouse nearby, a woman was walking toward her. A woman who lived here, not a tourist; it was easy to tell. She had the look of being comfortable, of being part of the land. A look that summer visitors never had. The men and women who owned the farms along this coast were rarely seen on the beach.

"Hi," said Eleanor. She wasn't sure she wanted to be interrupted.

"You staying over at Parker's?" the woman said. She settled beside Eleanor and dangled her legs over the edge of the cliff. "Parker's tourists come and go all summer but I hardly ever get to meet them. That's my farm just along the rise. This, too." She said it matter-of-factly and swept her arms to encompass the land around them. Eleanor guessed the woman to be in her sixties, sixty-two, sixty-three.

"Do you ever get used to this?" Eleanor pointed to the water, the beach. The coast unfurled before them; the cormorants had become still, perched high on the hoodoo.

"Believe it or not, there are times when I take it for granted," the woman said. "We're all guilty of that. But there isn't one of us up here, who'd leave." She grinned. "Once a week, I take a walk along here...strange things get swept in on the tide, you'd be astonished. Not," she said, "from the fishermen. There isn't a fisherman on this coast who'd drop so much as a paper plate over the side of his boat. If there's garbage on the boats they put it in a bag and bring it back to shore."

The woman's neck was wrinkled, a softness of red folds. Eleanor suddenly wanted to say to her: *I don't know what to do. When I found out, the first thing I did was go home. I took off my clothes and lay face down on the bathroom floor and banged my abdomen over and over and over against the hard tiles.* She wanted to tell a stranger that she had tried to—what? Dislodge it? Fiona's great-grandma had known better: *If you're meant to have it, you won't budge it with a stick of dynamite.* Later, Eleanor had lain on the cold floor, very still.

"Sometimes," the woman said, "I climb down these steps and walk as close as I can get to the caves over there under the cliffs. I put my nose right up to them and smell. Smell the red cliffs and the brine and the rock and the sea. I've never told that to my husband," she said. "He'd say I was foolish." She paused, watching the birds. "Sometimes, I come here just to sit. Right on this spot at the top of the steps where we are now...and I look out at that big rock. The night my daughter was born—she's a teacher in Alberta now—was the night of the worst storm to hit the Island in a hundred and forty years. That rock broke off from the mainland the night my daughter was born. Yes." She nodded her head as if to prove it were true. "Look at it now," she said. "It's so far out you'd never know it had once been connected."

The cormorants lifted and then settled again.

"It's all a mystery to me," she said, and pulled herself up. "You wouldn't believe how long it's taken me to learn that. It's taken even longer to learn to leave it alone." She placed her hand on Eleanor's shoulder—a firm pat. "I have to keep my bones moving," she said. "If you'd like to visit, come on over some day. I'm pretty well always at home."

Eleanor waited until the woman's figure had sunk below the fold in the hill. She was sorry she hadn't asked the woman's name. She eased herself down the steps to the beach and looked about, wondering if anyone were watching, not knowing why she should care. The woman's husband? If he saw her would he think Eleanor foolish, too? For she went directly to the shallow caves the woman had pointed out, and edged herself in as far as she could. Long wet sea grass was tucked far back, on shelves Eleanor could not reach. Salt had evaporated on the walls and linings of the caves. And there was moss. Thick moss that kept the surface both soft and dull.

Robert was in the big farm kitchen, trying to get a picture on the old black and white TV. Cass was outside holding her arms to the wind, making sails of her sleeves. She was wearing her bathing-suit under her shirt; her legs were skinny and brown.

"I was thinking," Robert said. "Maybe it's a pack rat in the walls. They do a lot of chewing." He was fiddling with wires and dials.

"Don't tell me that, just when I'm used to the idea of mice," Eleanor said, though she wasn't. She'd planned to tell Robert about meeting the woman but now she changed her mind.

Robert gave up and went out to take Cass for a swim. As soon as he left, the chewing began again, this time in the ceiling.

"You couldn't wait until nighttime, could you!" Eleanor shouted upward at empty space. She grabbed the broom handle and banged it against a ceiling tile. The noise stopped. "Thank you," she said.

Later in the day she found tiny chunks of ceiling and smaller fragments like sawdust sprinkled into her shawl, which she'd draped over a kitchen chair. She looked up and saw a hole the size of a quarter in the ceiling tile. The gnawed bits clung to the black fringe and she had to take the shawl to the verandah to shake it out. She closed her eyes while she shook because she didn't want to watch rodent droppings fall out.

From the verandah the earth was entirely yellow: the verandah boards, the half-harvested fields, the sand in the early evening light. A hawk, a white strip fanned across its spread tail, was hunting. It opened its wings and drifted easily in the wind, and disappeared over the top of the old house.

Again Eleanor stayed up late, reading. As soon as the house was silent, squeaks began in the wall closest to her. It was the gnawing, though, that was unbearable. Eleanor kicked the wall into silence. Seconds later the rodents moved to the ceiling. She banged at them with the broom handle but they were becoming braver.

41

Robert heard or felt her getting into bed and spoke her name. She wasn't certain if he were asleep or awake and her body tensed.

"Too much company for you out there, Eleanor?" he said.

"I banged the ceiling," she said, "and a body-part stuck out of the hole." Before he could ask, she said, "Don't."

She felt Robert's arm slide under her pillow. She thought of being in the cave, of pulling a blanket of sea grass up over her thighs and belly. She kept blotting her tears with the sheet.

"It's all right," he said. "It's all right. Whatever you decide, Eleanor, will be all right."

She thought for a moment that he, too, was crying.

She tossed in and out of Robert's arms and heard rattling as if the fridge were crepitating across the kitchen floor. Her dreams were mangled, confused; she woke in the dark and could not retrieve any part of them. She checked her watch— just after three in the morning. She looked at Robert and thought of his arm sliding under her, the words that lay unspoken between them, the mice chewing steadily in the walls and ceiling, probably running across the floor after she and Robert had fallen asleep. She was no longer sure of what could and could not be said, of what was best left unspoken. She thought of the woman on the cliff, of the mystery. It had taken a long time to learn to leave it alone, the woman had said. What exactly had she meant? Eleanor knew that if she had to ask, she would never understand. *Could* never understand.

She slid out of bed and closed the bedroom door behind her. Thinking of mice, she switched on a kitchen light. She wrapped herself in her black shawl and on a whim decided to go out and stand in the night.

She stepped off the verandah and tilted her head back. And without faltering allowed the sudden wonder, the excitement, the awareness of what had silently encircled her. She thought of waking Robert so this could be shared, and decided, *No,* and

42

of Cass, and if only Cass could...and then, *No*, again. Barefoot, she made her way across sand and grass to the blackest part of the cliff, away from the artificial glow spilling from the kitchen window.

Light rose and fell from a giant dome that filled the sky. She was surrounded by, she was at the centre of great vertical sheets of light. It encompassed her, illuminated the sky as she stood. She wanted to believe that she was hearing the Chorus, too, its music pitched higher than a steady hum. One note, but rising, rising, never descending. She was at the centre of all of this—light, sound, the sky consummately clear, brighter than it could ever be with a full moon.

Wisps of cloud seemed to sweep and gather above her but even as she watched, these began to disperse and blow out over the sea. The lights, played out, gave way to more and more cloud. She did not know how long she'd been standing in that spot—minutes? hours? She became aware of cold, penetrating her feet and legs. Her muscles were stiff, her feet cramped against the sand. She thought of Cass and Robert, warm and silent in their rooms in the yellow house. She was alone but not alone, part of them and part of this, too. And her unborn child, was it aware of the dark sea swirling below? Of the clouds rushing away with the fading Chorus?

Eleanor shifted her body and moved to go back toward the yellow house. But because she'd stayed so long in the blackest part of the cliff, because the sea had crept where it never came by day, because she knew the child was stirring inside her— she paused, and stretched out her arms, confused for that brief moment, about which way the earth was turning.

An August Wind

An August wind had lashed the coast for three days; not a single blue-and-white fishing-boat had been seen on the horizon throughout that time.

A great white shark, weighing a ton, had drowned seven miles out in the cod nets four days before, and had been hauled to Covehead where its seventeen-foot length now hung by its tail from a hoist in the harbour so that people could ogle and touch, and take photographs. The wide teeth had been hacked from it, to be sold, and its mouth, gaping and slack, dragged the ground while fishermen stood round, arms folded, impatient to get back to their nets but glad of this diversion, which relieved the monotony of their idleness, their enforced obedience to the wind.

The sun had shone through three days of wind and was shining still on stray groups of swimmers up the coast who had placed towels and blankets in the shelter of the red cliffs. Close to shore, on dark sand that was lapped intermittently, a damsel-fly struggled on its side; its linear black body, its beaded head, had been crushed by some mishap of nature. Helen disturbed two sandpipers running side by side as she jumped through the waves, hearing Valerie's screams that the wind had kept from her, then, had brought in a rush, flooding her ears. There was no thought in her mind as she flung herself through shallow surf, no thought but, "Valerie, Valerie!" The sandpipers waited until she had passed; they stood, immobile as herons, as the lash of a small wave overturned pebbles, created new eddies that the birds probed hurriedly for a meal of sandcrabs. They scurried up the shore, away from the people now running along the beach. They stopped, waited, then quickened their slender curved beaks to a rhythm slightly faster than the sudden shadows of their prey.

The old woman sat on a lawnchair at the top of the red cliff; her craggy face was swept in the wind by threads of her own white hair. Long ago, in a spring-swollen pond, someone had drowned, a stone around the neck. She looked down on the scene below and saw the child floundering as she screamed, where the surf became higher, where breakers tossed her, like a rag.

The sands were frantic with the activity of decay. With each large wave came other rippling, shallow waves, creating rivulets between humps of sand formed that day by sea and wind. Each movement set another in motion, causing water to

45

trill over sandbars from three or four directions, crisscrossing, equalizing until every droplet rejoined the sea.

Up from the waves, the sand had begun to dry but was still somewhat hardened and packed. Sand fleas, patterned like flicking doilies, created circles around upturned washed-in skates whose flat fishy moulds seemed to be made of white rubber, their long tails extended behind. Toward the dunes the sand was loose and pale; here large crabs had been swept by earlier waves or by wind or had crawled out of the ocean or had been dropped by gulls. And now they lay on their backs, their fleshy green-white undersides exposed, their bent legs loosened, sometimes strewn helter skelter about the sand.

Helen was in deeper water now, the surf trying to pitch her back to shore. She swam and the rhythm of her arms with each stroke cried, "Valerie, Valerie!" She had almost reached the child who, seeing her mother, began to try again; her weakened strokes brought her to Helen who directed the child toward shore. Then Helen gathered her strength and tried to follow Valerie in.

The old woman on the cliff nodded. She turned her head and faced the flat open beach which was unprotected by cliffs— where the man in black swimming-trunks had run and was shouting: for rope, for a boat, for rescue.

Wind lifted the sand and drove it to sea; lifted it in fine visible manes that tossed their silky, slithering traces. And then, the wind turned, came down from the north and raised the breakers until they were over Helen's head by fifteen inches. The undertow began to suck at her legs and fought with the surf for her body. Valerie had been caught up by shore waves and had reached safety. The men who were halfway to Helen now turned back, crawled up on the beach, exhausted by the new current that was tugging Helen out to sea. She was pushed

46

toward shore by one wave, dragged out farther by the next. Valerie, the man in black swimming-trunks helping her, struggled to her feet on the beach, unaware that she had, mercifully, stepped on the thread-like neck of the damsel-fly. Its struggle ended, it now washed out to sea.

On the beach, weed and dulse, sea lettuce and Irish moss had twisted and tangled during three days of erratic relentless wind. High soft heaps of decay were gradually covered over, packed down. Whiskery tufts of weed clung to half-opened mussels; slipper shells attached themselves to the hard blue curve. Limpets stuck like Oriental hard-hats to slipper shells, never to be pried away. Under the waves, barnacles opened and froze like yawning molars as they were swept to shore. All suffered the pounding of wind. Lashing, lifting, stinging wind.

The long grasses along the rise of the dunes bent, yielding, but never released their grip beneath the sand. On top of the red cliffs the soil was covered with dry stubble. In the curvatures just below the edge, cliff swallows rested in chains of circular nests, watchful, waiting for early evening when they would crisscross one another's flights like swooping bats.

Thistles and hard close weeds grew then, from the top of the cliffs, grew under the chair of the old woman with the craggy face, back, back to soil which, still red, became lush, and fertile. A bumblebee was thrown off course again and again in the changing wind—now from land, now from sea. The bee swerved crazily, flying low to the grass where the old woman sat, looking down to the sea.

The waves knocked at Helen's head until she cried in pain, "Stop!" They knocked at her again and again as bright flashing lights danced before her eyes. She thought she saw Valerie in the big yellow towel, standing with the ring of people on

47

shore, and she said to herself, "So many, all staring at me." But closed her eyes and when she opened them, tried to relieve the pain at the back of her head. She was almost grateful that her vision had clouded and she could not see. She tried, though she could not, to move her neck so she would be able to hear the boat that would come from the side, to save her.

The waves cracked and knocked at the foot of the cliff; there was no boat that day. The old woman on the cliff could have told them that; she could see in both directions all along the coast. The nearest boats had been pulled up high in the fishing village; the wind had only tightened the knots in the ropes that held them. The wind kept the fishermen muttering, their arms folded.

Again and again, Helen's toes tipped against a sandbar; then, she lost even that in the sway. The wind rode hard on the waves. Though she could not see them coming from behind, she knew the precise moment each would roll over her head. She held the rhythm now, of dying. She tried to close her mouth and hold her breath with each wave, thinking, "Not yet, not yet you won't, not yet." And felt and heard water gurgling in her throat, though she had not spoken aloud. "I can't hold on, but not yet." She had stopped hoping that the boat would come. She could not see the shore because of the cloud in her eyes. She felt for the sand with her toes again and kept her arms at her side when she could, to keep the heaviness from her shoulders. "I am drowning," she allowed herself to say. "Valerie was turned back and if she is not wanted too then she is safe on shore. I am drowning, and she is safe on shore." And once more, she said, "Valerie, Valerie."

The old woman pointed to the ropes as they ran up the path of the cliff; the men flung the ropes down and tied them, even the clothesline that had been strung out beside the vacant barn at the end of the field. The knots jerked and held; clothespins and colourfully braided fishing ropes sailed on the waves, out and out, a child's gay purple raft bobbing at the end. The men and women made a chain—two with the raft, one at each section of line. The old woman watched the wooden clothespins tip into the sea.

Zebra-striped wings of seabirds wagged saucily on currents of wind. Heavy casual gulls soared, crying pit-a-tree pit-a-tree scree scree scree. With this last cry they dived through frothy caps of the highest waves, ducking out again as the waves furled and reached for the softness of their necks.

Helen lay on the beach and accepted the warmth of blankets and the bright yellow towel. She heard voices as men and women stooped over her. She was carried up the path to the ambulance, which had backed as far as it could down the clay road. The old woman nodded; she lifted herself from the chair and began the slow walk back to her farm.

In early evening the wind shrugged and lowered its shoulder. Boats pushed off from the harbour; fishermen waved to one another as their small vessels chugged out of the bay in a steady purposeful line. The nets would be inspected; perhaps, if damage was slight, an evening catch hauled in.

The sun-rotted carcass of the great white shark was towed back to sea where it was cut free from the little boat; and was torn at and ogled as it sank past its fellow creatures.

Just before sun began to set, each blade of marram grass was still; each blade gleamed in the last bright light so that together, all of the grasses covered the curves of hills and dunes like clumps of sparkling diamonds.

Copper Kettle

By chance, the road leads them to the copper-market town of Villedieu-les-Poëles. Sue Ellen wants to stop for coffee so they park the car and pick their way down cobbled streets until they find a tiny but dark café between market stalls. An old woman sits at a booth; a *baguette* protrudes from a basket beside her. She exchanges looks with the woman behind the bar.

"*Les touristes*," says the old woman softly, as if the tourists themselves cannot hear.

"*Américains*," replies the other and turns back to her work.

The American war graves are not far up the road. Field upon field of crosses carved from Carrara marble.

Gabe, who wears light sports trousers, a turtleneck and white shoes, takes the observer's seat: the chair that provides the view of what is going on, who enters, who departs. Gabe, the social worker, has been in the profession so long he says he's run out of fresh responses. When he works with his cases he reverses what is said to him, and hands the statements back. He sometimes does this to Sue Ellen, deliberately or not, she doesn't know. When her own mother was dying, he stood outside the hospital room and said, "And how do you feel about that?" They'd both been shocked at the way this had come out but he'd tried to cover up. "One of the hazards of the trade," he sometimes jokes. "Clichés. One begins to think one has seen and heard it all."

Beside Gabe sits nine-year old Melanie. She is a late child, born to them after seven years of trying. Gabe thinks Melanie is like Sue Ellen and therefore, since he's made the comparison, unlike him. Her mannerisms, certain ways she has of looking up, of turning quickly from the side, catch him off guard. In fact, if the truth were known, he's always been uneasy around her. The lines of her eyes, for instance, droop from the outer corners and this gives her the look of one who is permanently insulted. There are times when her appearance is that of a slouched, brooding child. Gabe thinks she sulks excessively but he sometimes overhears her and Sue Ellen laughing from different parts of the house, so he has to allow for a sense of humour that does not include him.

"While we're here, Melanie," Gabe finds himself saying, to his own surprise, "let's buy your mother a copper kettle." His hands sweep up and out as if by way of explanation or apology. "Isn't tomorrow her birthday? Isn't this the copper centre of Normandy?" He has read this latter fact on a sign at the edge of town.

Melanie peers at him through drooping eyes. Sue Ellen is not enthusiastic. She's past the acquisitive stage and is not one to pick up souvenirs or waste time shopping in the towns of Europe. But even while she argues she begins to shift her ground; the idea of a gift of copper pleases her though she knows that the gesture is conciliatory and that she will not forgive Gabe. Still, some measure of her yearns for peace, old times, things the way they used to be. The way she now sees them as they used to be. Before Rose? After Rose? Difficult to say. There are complications, real memories that thwart her efforts to simplify the past.

Gabe leads the way, feeling benevolent and even powerful. He knows that Sue Ellen has not been entirely happy; with a grand inner gesture he swears to himself that he'll make it up to her. They begin to compare pots and kettles of every shape and size, down the market hill, back up the other side, in and out of crammed and tiny showrooms. But Sue Ellen does not seem to be able to make up her mind. She begins to sing softly as they drag their way up and down stone steps:

Get you a copper kettle
Get you a copper coil
Cover with new-made corn mash
And nevermore you'll toil

Melanie takes her mother's hand and hums along at her side. Gabe ignores this thread of light-heartedness that binds the women of his family, and looks at his watch. It's his responsibility to see that they stick to schedule. Who knows where they'll end up spending the night? He's calculated that they should be able to get to Reims. He begins to grind his teeth, a sound he's unaware of creating. Sue Ellen has been expecting this gnashing of teeth. Not only can she predict with some precision the moment at which it will begin, she can even, at certain perverse moments, provoke it.

It is not a new kettle but an old one that Sue Ellen finally chooses. An antique, a wide-brimmed marmalade kettle, warm-coloured copper, smooth and deep with sturdy handles—a kettle too vast to fit over a burner on a North American stove. But even as Gabe pays for it and presents it to Sue Ellen, she knows that she will never use it for marmalade. She will never stand for hours shredding rind to paper-thin slivers, she will never nick her fingertips, boil fruit or pulp, pick out seeds. No, she will plunk a geranium into her finely hammered copper and she will push it toward the sun.

If Sue Ellen hadn't taken so long to make up her mind at the market, they wouldn't be looking for a hotel now, so far from Reims. She knows this is what Gabe is thinking, so she's careful to be optimistic when she thinks she sees the outline of a town ahead. Normandy is far behind. They are between Paris and Reims, the heavily-trafficked route of the industrial northeast. Sue Ellen and Gabe have learned the hazards of looking for hotels after dark. If they're to find a place at all they'll have to leave the highway and enter one of the depressing grey towns linked every twenty kilometres or so all the way to Reims. In Reims, the scenery will become beautiful again. They'll visit the cathedral in the morning. The landscape will become forested and hilly. And after that, they will recross the border into Germany where rigidity will clarify itself and cleanliness of washroom can be counted on. They'll head for Frankfurt where they'll return the rented Passat. And they'll fly home.

Gabe is grinding his teeth. Sue Ellen interprets this to mean that he is impatient for her and her unerring intuition to say, "Quick, this is it. Get ready to turn." She does, in fact, say just that and they settle back, edgy, hungry, but willing to follow this dilatory turn of events.

Actually, Sue Ellen's ability to find restaurants and hotels in unlikely places is accurate to the point of being disturbing. Gabe wonders, but never questions. It's a part of Sue Ellen he does not comprehend. It's as if she has chosen to be this way, as one would choose obstinacy, for instance.

Melanie, in the back seat, stares hard out the window and

delivers herself of an aggrieved sniffle. It's nearly eight in the evening, a dusky hour of her mother's birthday eve. Rain is falling from a morbid and unattractive sky. Behind the windshield wipers neither Gabe nor Sue Ellen removes the heavily smoked prescription glasses each wears as the car leaves the main road and veers off to the right.

A sheath of soot might have been pulled in one taut piece over every structure of this town. Not a citizen is to be seen. Not a citizen, bush, flower, not a stroke of fresh paint.

"Jesus, what a dispiriting place." Gabe gnashes his teeth as he cruises up and down, coming quickly to a street that gapes onto an uncultivated field. He reverses gears and they drive back through the town, searching the streets house by house.

In her head, Sue Ellen hums the tune she sang in the market, this time changing the words:

He gives you a copper kettle
He gives you a band of gold

It is Melanie who spots the restaurant, though at the same moment Sue Ellen sees the word *Hôtel* and the single star sunken into the outer wall of a two-storey building, which looks as if it might be the front of a cement factory. Sue Ellen is relieved, pleased at the way things are turning out. A hotel with one star. A find. A miracle.

Behind the fence, sounds of pounding and hammering can be heard. Sue Ellen the practised room-finder rings the front bell again and again while Gabe and Melanie remain in the car, foreheads wrinkled behind glass as they peer through the rain.

The shouts stop (later, upstairs, Sue Ellen will say this was in disbelief) and the front door opens with a yank. Three children of varying states of dress stare at her and set up a cry over their shoulders. "*Maman!*" *Maman* leads Sue Ellen upstairs to a faded yellow room with sink and shower cubicle buckled into a far wall. *Maman* stays discreetly outside the doorway looking off into the dim hall. Sue Ellen, knowing better than to look too closely, accepts the room.

Outside, the wooden fence suddenly splits in two, and a heretofore unseen gate opens onto a crumbling courtyard, which in any other country would be a garden. There are heaps of stone and gravel, old hoses, a cement mixer. Two monstrous German shepherds hurl themselves against the car as Gabe inches into the grounds. The gate slams and locks behind them. A man and a boy signal them to leave the car, and collar the dogs, which continue to lunge. Melanie and Sue Ellen run for the door while Gabe collects the overnight bag. They are conducted the back way, into a narrow kitchen, past a chipped countertop and a deep stone sink that contains clumps of unwashed chicory; through a wide and spacious dining-room, up the stairs and "*Voilà.*"

Gabe looks about but is prudent enough to keep his own counsel. Melanie runs across the room and claims her bed, a single by the wall of the shower cubicle. Will *Madame et Monsieur* be taking dinner? They nod. No other restaurant exists. *Maman* withdraws. Sue Ellen sighs and goes to the window where she separates cobwebbed curtains that droop from a high plaster ceiling. Gabe, unaware, is grinding his teeth again...*Rrrr Rrrr Rrrr.*

Lately, Sue Ellen has begun to consider herself a fraud. Not only does she recognize this imposture before herself, but also before Melanie. As for Gabe, he's not easily duped and knows more about her than she cares to think about. But it's Melanie she worries about. Melanie has a tendency to exaggerate her mother's strengths and Sue Ellen feels that in moments of hypocrisy, she has even encouraged this. Sometimes she wonders what Melanie would think if she were to know what really went on. What if she were told about Rose? What would she think of Gabe? How when he was alone the one weekend she and Melanie had left to visit Sue Ellen's father, he'd had Rose in the house; how Sue Ellen had found a size six, high-heeled shoe in his closet, the day after they returned. It didn't help that Sue Ellen herself wore tens.

A shoe? she'd shrieked. *A tiny shoe? How did she make her getaway, hop home on one foot?*

What would anyone think if it were known that Sue Ellen had cried every night for weeks after Gabe had carefully left his clues around. Not cried, wailed. Carrying on like a demented and pathetic creature, even after Gabe had escaped into sleep. If Gabe now knows the parameters of her desperation, it's too late to make alterations. The problem is, Sue Ellen has become exhausted while trying to direct and maintain this unbroken rage. This wears her down more than the knowledge of Gabe's infidelity itself. Also, she knows little about this woman except what Gabe has chosen to tell. That Rose is a colleague, also a social worker; that she works at the Veterans' Hospital, across the parking lot and through the tunnel from the General where Gabe has his office; that she is childlike and earnest, that she has timid eyes, that she *needs* him. In lighter moments Sue Ellen imagines Gabe and Rose having earnest but clichéd conversations over hospital coffee and luncheon curry.

"Do you think she found my little shoe, Gabe?"

"What makes you think she found your little shoe, Rose?"

"Does she know about us?"

"She knows your shoe size. And how do you feel about that?"

"It worries me. I'm worried about her."

"Would you like to share those feelings with me, Rose?"

Does Gabe still see Rose? Sue Ellen is not certain. It was Gabe's idea to take the European holiday, to drive through parts of West Germany and France. There has been no mention of Rose.

Of course, Sue Ellen could leave. She stands before the mirror every morning and tells herself this. She and Melanie could pack their bags and walk away and there would be nothing Gabe could do.

Or Gabe could leave. Sue Ellen has imagined the details of this. The day she found the shoe she told him to go.

But she and Gabe had pulled back when she said this and nothing more that day was said or done. It was as if each were immobilized by the vision of a final and even possible, separating act.

Perhaps they simply don't have the good grace to face what their marriage is. She wonders if that is not the entire problem. Does Gabe feel, as she sometimes does, that there will no longer be change or adventure in their lives? She could look for a lover but she would have to pay more attention to her appearance, lose a few pounds, buy some new clothes. She could iron the sheets to make the bed more attractive. She could wear a piece of *Saran* when she greets Gabe in the evening. She feels an uncontrollable urge to go out of control. If men are going to want her, they are going to have to want her the way she is.

She turns away from the window, refusing to look at the dirt on the sill, and catches Gabe's eye as she lets the curtain fall. He grins, and shrugs at the squalor. And with this sudden exchange, they enter a momentary truce. Despite her anger and his response to her anger, sometimes they cannot help themselves falling into these temporary states, these gestures of intimacy and permanence. And being unsure is not only the lot of Sue Ellen. There have been times, recent times, when Gabe has looked shaken. It's as if some part of him suddenly becomes fragile and vulnerable and he is threatened by the fulfilment of an uncertain prognostication. Yes, he looks physically shaken.

At five minutes to nine, Gabe, Sue Ellen and Melanie descend to the dining-room. The children of the household are seated at a table at the far end of this enormous room, waiting. Bangs and shouts can still be heard from the back of the house.

The curious thing about the dining-room is that tables have been prepared as if to receive some 60 or 70 people. Each is draped with a brown tablecloth and thick yellow serviettes that someone has taken the trouble to shape into cones and stand on end by each plate. Each table holds a vase and a fresh white flower. The children of the house watch their guests closely and jerk their heads in laughter at every move. Except for the fresh flowers, the room might be set for company on the eve of the First Great War. Sue Ellen thinks of the single star carved in cement on the outer wall and tries to imagine who, if anyone, awarded the honour.

Gabe blurts out between his teeth, "Jesus, look at them, Sue Ellen. Just look at them. They all have the same pasty-faced look. Bad nutrition, hand-me-down clothes." He sighs in the attitude of Gabe the social worker. "The thorns in the sides of the poor. If this were my case, I'd be out there inspecting the kitchen; it's probably crawling with vermin."

But he goes ahead and orders one of two possibilities on the menu—beefsteak—and Melanie says she'll have the same.

At this moment, the man of the house, one of the pounders and hammerers, sticks his round face into the dining room and shouts, *"Salutations!"* before ducking back to the kitchen. His children find this uproariously funny, and double over, the eldest even diving beneath the table in splutters and moans of laughter.

The meal is served. Sue Ellen has ordered something she considers safe, a plain rice dish in which she finds a hair. But there is an unexpected turn in what Gabe has now begun to call their *fleabag adventure*. During the second course, a loud *Hurrah!* sounds from the back followed by a roar of descending plaster, a gush of water, total silence. Even the children across the room are stunned. *Maman* comes solemnly into the room, stands at the edge of the table and says with some sadness to Sue Ellen, "The pipe has burst. We shall have no water until tomorrow. I'm sorry, but I must find you another hotel."

Gabe begins to shake. Melanie, seeing her father and hearing the unmistakable sounds of a wide broom sweeping water, giggles uncontrollably.

"It looks as if we can escape after all," says Sue Ellen, translating brightly, facing *Maman*. "The pipe has burst!"

But another hotel? Here, in this town? *Maman* nods her head and leaves the room. She returns, smiling. *"Voilà!"* says she. "You won't have to leave, after all. The pipe is fixed."

In the morning, *Maman* is angry because her guests refuse to stay for *petit déjeuner*. The rolls were ordered the night before; they'll be delivered and no-one will be here to eat them. But no, Sue Ellen is firm. It is her birthday. The gate must be opened; the dogs must be held.

The husband, in undershirt and pyjama bottoms, bangs downstairs, grumbling and swearing while he holds the dogs. Sue Ellen and Melanie refuse to go into the backyard, and wait for Gabe to drive out to the street before they get into the car.

As they drive through the streets of Reims searching for breakfast near the cathedral, Gabe announces that he's going to be sick. It must have been the meat, last night. It had a strange taste. He should have known better than to touch meat in a fleabag. Melanie says she's getting a funny feeling in her stomach. Just as they park and walk around to the entrance of the cathedral, Melanie throws up on the stones outside, and promptly feels better. They decide to visit the cathedral later, and they cross the street, entering a clean and wonderful café. Gabe runs for the *Messieurs* while a man behind the bar, wiping glasses, shakes his head sadly. Sue Ellen takes Melanie to the washroom and they scrub. They scrub arms and faces, hands and nails with soap and hot water, trying to remove both dirt and memory of the one-star hotel. And sit for an hour over a breakfast of steaming coffee, chocolate and croissants with marmalade.

It is in such a place that Sue Ellen would have wished to wake on her birthday morn. It would have been little to ask— a clean bed, a fresh roll. But no, she has begun her new year in a fleabag. There is no escaping this truth. She woke in a drooped and lumpy bed watching spiders spin back to their corner webs. And lay quietly, remembering the night before.

They'd returned to their room after dinner, but would not use the water in the sink because of the filth around the drain and taps. Gabe volunteered to run the gauntlet past the dogs, to bring Vichy from the car. The toilet, down the hall, was dirtier than the sink. Melanie, infected by the gloom of her parents, stumbled around by the light of the ceiling bulb, and prepared for bed.

Sue Ellen brushed her teeth with Vichy, turned out the light, and settled Melanie on the far side of the room. She groped back through the dark and parted the curtains, before climbing into bed beside Gabe.

She knew that when Gabe had gone downstairs to the car he'd brought back not only the Vichy, but also the copper kettle. Its broad base rested on the wide sill, and reflected a flame-hued glow, from the sky, or the street below, or from a wisp of moon that offered a glimpse of itself between the curtains. Perhaps Gabe meant it as a renewed offering, the ageing but beautiful kettle. Something to greet Sue Ellen's eyes on her birthday morn. She lay there, and remembering the song, rearranged the lines again, in her head:

> He gives you a copper kettle
> He gives you a band of gold

Long ago, she'd accepted a band of gold from Gabe. A clear winter's day, and they'd believed that their happiness would last forever.

Sue Ellen thought of Rose. And lay on her back, allowing a depression so heavy she knew it could not be overcome. After a long silence, Gabe's voice lifted out of the darkness beside her.

"Do you think, Sue Ellen," asked the voice, "do you think

that before you inspected this room, you could have been dazzled by the star?"

And they began to laugh. On a thin mattress that sagged almost to the floor and upon which they could not prevent themselves rolling to the middle, they laughed. Staring up at the ceiling, they shook until the bed shook and the whole floor shook and their eyes filled with tears that overran their pillows. Melanie joined in from the far side of the room, her childish laughter hiccuping uncertainly through the dark. And when Sue Ellen felt Gabe's arms around her she continued to shake, not knowing if she were on the verge of revelation or humility, awareness or pretence, illumination or darkness.

Touches

You know you've been led to a table in the annex, the closed-in verandah, because you are alone. It's not so bad. You prefer this to the dining-room into which you can look back from an inner window beside your table. The outer windows allow a view of the grounds, the river, the uneven hill, a thicket beside three very old trees, the trunks of which you'd never be able to wrap your arms around.

There are two men in the annex, each at a single table in this narrow verandah; places have been discreetly set so that their backs are presented to you. You can only guess at their faces.

This is fine with you. You've come here to be alone.

The dining-room is half-filled—it's off-season—and from time-to-time you glance up from your meal to look back in through the open window. It's easy to overhear conversations because most of the occupants of the dining-room are elderly and speak in loud voices. You, who are half their age, assume that hearing is a problem.

By far, the loudest of these is Bert, whose name you've been forced to learn. Bert not only has a hearing problem, he has misplaced his reading-glasses. He glares across the room directly at you, as it turns out, while his wife reads aloud tonight's menu. You and everyone else in the annex and the dining-room must now listen to the naming of each item followed by Bert shouting it back to his wife:

"Beef?"

"NOT BEEF."

"Sautéed veal?"

"I don't like that. You know I HATE EEL."

"Mexican Shrimp?"

"Yes! That's what I'll have. PEMMICAN SHRIMP."

There is another couple at Bert's table, fellow travellers, the silent kind, suffering. Probably from Bert's behaviour. You know a suffering face when you see one. Your entire professional life so far has been spent with sufferers.

You ban this thought from your head and pull a paperback from your shoulder bag, *The Beginning of Spring*, by Penelope Fitzgerald. You like this book because it's about a hearty Russian family and the unsealing of the windows in spring. All the dreary winter, the promise of unsealing the windows is held before an assortment of rowdy characters through a complicated series of entanglements. You hope that at the end of the story, everyone, including you, will experience the thrusting open of heavy panes of glass in stifling rooms, that everyone will feel the rushing in of spring.

Bert is now roaring at his wife: "I don't see one thing funny about your joke. Not one thing!" His face contorts in anger and he glares first at his wife, and then at you, because he sees you looking. He leaves his table and stomps out of the dining-room. You tell yourself he's an old poot, you've met plenty, that you and everyone else will probably have to listen to him all week because you all have better manners than he does.

You like your second-storey room, though it's at the side of the lodge, a less-than-choice location. The water is visible only as flashes of blue through the trees. An oak presses against your window; its leaves are green and new and large but they have a touch of red, too, as if they might deceive and turn into fall maples, instead. It's early June and you smell river. There is a weedy bank, a dock, an ancient smell that you know well. It's the smell of underwater, of rock unturned, of fish and weed and riverbank all mingled together.

You think of Louisa, who is the same age as your Zoe, seven. Louisa, of the tiny-boned face and the beautiful name. You approach slowly though you have known Louisa for months; you sit next to her in a room at the Children's Aid. Louisa's pupils dilate, ready. You watch some part of her scurry inside herself. After a few moments, after listening to your voice, she lifts your hand and holds it between her own small palms as if she is the adult and you are the child. She lets your hand drop, nods her head wisely and says, "I don't think I'll talk about *that*." She gets up from her chair and goes to the window. She seems to be humming, humming behind closed lips. When she turns, her pupils are normal again. You think, *Okay, good.* A tiny if imperceptible gain.

Later, you go to a place provided by the court where you meet Louisa's mother, and you have a long session with her. When you return to your office, Becky, who is also a Psychologist, brings you a cup of strong tea and walks you three times around the block. You and Becky are honed to rescue each other, to recognize each other's breaking point. Becky is your closest friend. Sometimes you say to her and she to you, mocking each other, "Identified the problem yet, dearie?" And you both laugh, grimly. So many problems are spilled out over the two of you, day after day.

You wonder why you've come to this lodge alone. Answers rise up easily: no holiday for over a year, caseload too heavy; space, you need space away from Alex and Zoe. You see Alex standing in the doorway at home. "I know you have to go," he says. "It's only for a week," you say. You bend forward to kiss Zoe, who stands beside Alex. She's wearing her yellow trousers and top and she looks like a buttercup and you feel like hugging her and hugging her and crying out that the world is not safe, be careful, for God's sake, take care, there's a whole world out there you know nothing about. But you kiss her and walk away calmly, even though your foot shakes over the pedal as you back the car out of the driveway. You will yourself, force yourself, to drive smoothly away.

Bert shouts to his wife but, clearly, he is aiming his voice at you. "That girl has been alone at her table ever since she got here!" You are a cast in Bert's eye. You, the 37-year-old girl, glance up from your book long enough to stare at Bert, eye-to-eye. The other three at his table murmur soothing remarks to calm his outburst.

"Why don't you invite her over," says Bert's wife, "if you're that concerned."

Through the annex window you hear his arguments as he backs down. Sometimes people want to sit alone, not like him, he says. Nosirree, he likes company, though he can be with himself for a little while. He musters his anger and shouts in your direction, "At least I'm not anti-social!"

The loons call out in the early evening and don't stop until long after dark. You listen from your second-storey window. You can hear young women in the kitchen below, the reassuring sounds of backroom life that keep the place going. Dishes scraped, cleaned, put away. Potatoes peeled, vegetables chopped for the next day. A screen-door slaps and an older woman's voice yells, "Where do you think you're going?" Next, there is the sound of a young man entering, a different sort of sound; the women's voices change. After that, a water fight. Laughter, more laughter and you find yourself smiling, upstairs in your tiny room. Amidst the laughter, the women eject the man from the kitchen.

You and Alex laugh like that sometimes. This thought presses in, the way the oak scrunches against the screen at your window.

Every morning before breakfast you walk along the river. You draw in the mixed scent of late spring and early summer. In the woods, there are birds: a woodpecker you hear every day but cannot see; baby robins, long-tailed swallows, geese straggling back toward their feeding grounds.

You hear Becky's voice. "Identified the problem yet, dearie? Would a fast walk help? A wailing wall? A hair-shirt?"

A rest, you answer, inside your head. Only a rest. That's all.

When you return to the lodge an elderly couple is sitting on one of the benches along the river path. They see you but are so immersed in argument they don't care. The man shouts at his wife who is close beside him, wrapped in her cardigan. "I want you to PROMISE me—on the Bible—that we won't FIGHT." The woman wheedles, cajoles, cannot be heard. She seems familiar with this role, does not object to the way he bullies her. He shouts again, discounting your presence, your ears. "Let me finish for Christ sake. PROMISE me we won't FIGHT!" You've not seen this couple before. They probably eat during second-sitting in the dining-room. You never see them again.

At lunch, Bert resumes his childlike rule over the table. "What do I like?" he says. "I like onions. Green onions. And radishes. I can eat radishes. But I can leave them alone, too."

He lists every vegetable he can think of, a long list that represents Bert's lifetime. It's as if what Bert's bowels can or cannot digest, past and present, is not only the loudest but the most interesting list anyone has ever heard. "I'm a fast eater, too," he says. "I've always been one to clean right up."

"This is our holiday," says Bert's wife, as if the very mention of vegetables does not belong here, at the lodge.

All of the diners at all of the other tables have run out of conversation at the same time.

You think of the last holiday at the Children's Aid, the Valentine party. You and Becky are at the party with other staff members, to help, observe, supervise games. You marvel as you watch the girls, watch the eight-year-olds dress and act as if they're sixteen. Makeup, long flashy earrings, high heels—these are not dress-ups. The girls are spirited as they tap deliberate messages in spiked heels, as they stride across the wooden floor and make too-frequent trips to the washroom. Becky, who knows what you're thinking, comes up behind you and says, "Who *buys* these shoes? Do the kids actually wear these to school?" You're both thinking, yes, they probably do.

The girls show off; they're in competition for attention from their case-workers, from you, from Becky, from the *boys*.

Louisa is at this party. She sticks to your side most of the time. You've told Becky, a long time ago, months ago, "This child is old."

An extra is needed for a team game and Louisa's name is called. Her head goes down bluntly. Her eyes film. An older girl—older? she might be nine instead of seven—calls out protectively, "Leave Louisa out, her father did gross touches to her. She doesn't feel like playing yet." The others, boys and girls alike, nod, knowing what *that* means. Nothing could have stopped the remark, no-one could have pulled it back. It's the language these ancient abused children live and know. When the party food is served, Louisa joins the others, laughing, reaching past shoulders and heads. Everyone is a little greedy, a little grabby. For a few minutes, over pink frosting and ice cream, you are fooled into believing they could be a group of normal kids.

Zoe comes home from her Grade 2 class, walks in the back door and sets down her schoolbag. "Today we learned SEX," she tells you. "The teacher read the same book we have at home. The school nurse was there, too. We learned how babies are made."

"Did you now?" you say, and grab her close for a hug.

Zoe pulls back so she can watch your face. "You know that time you and Dad made me," she says, "when he had to put his penis in you? Well, when he put it inside you, did he burst out laughing?"

You and Alex *clutch* each other in laughter over that. Behind your closed bedroom door. Later, several weeks later, Zoe tells you—again she waits until the two of you are alone—"I'm never going to let any man put his thing in *me*."

She looks really miffed at the idea.

There's no answer to that, you decide, safely.

Every day you walk farther and farther from the lodge. You've met the dogs on the farms, and when you're in the woods you're not afraid of bears. A humming sort of heat has descended; a profusion of dragonflies and bees, of poison ivy, thick along the edge of the dirt road. There are strawberry plants and even honeysuckle, which you've not seen for a long time.

You are as silent as you hope to be.

You think of Alex. Now that you are away you can't keep yourself from tallying up. You know that the two of you can live together for months, asking nothing except that each is there for the other. It's as if you truly believe that marriage, life, is that simple.

It is.

Then, some urgent need for discord rears itself, gnaws up the side of you, takes form in the shape of impatience, irritation, anger.

High tide and low.

Alex always wants to wait things out. As if time is on his side, as if you both have all the time in the world. You—you admit this to yourself—want to delve to the heart, you want to *identify the problem*. But just as quickly as it has dissolved, peace reasserts itself. Fingers reach across a desert sheet. A cold toe brushes against a bare leg. You are learning and so is Alex. In your separate system of beliefs, you are learning to leave alone what must be left alone, that debris will always be present, waterlogged, beneath the surface.

Louisa says she would like to move into your house and live with you. You cannot adopt her, bring her into your circle of safety, though you would if you could. Louisa has a home, whatever it may be. Louisa's mother watched Louisa's father as he did gross touches. She was forced to; some part of Louisa doesn't know this. Now, Louisa's father is not allowed to be in or near the apartment building where Louisa and her mother live. Louisa tells you that he will be arrested if he puts a toe on the grass in front of the building. You continue to see Louisa twice a week but that is all you can do.

You enter the dining-room. Bert is waiting. He sees that you are carrying a book, a different one this time. He shouts out as you cross the room to get to the annex, "What does she come here for, to READ?" You stick in Bert's craw like the bone in the wolf's throat. No-one at his table can explain you. "Why don't you *ask* her why she comes here," says Bert's wife. But he does not. Instead, he complains loudly and bitterly throughout the meal. You ask yourself if the men of his generation were born angry.

Becky has a theory that entire generations of men have been

brought up to believe it's their divine right to be listened to. She's put in her years, she says, of listening to opinionated men. Once a month, you and Becky go out for dinner after work. One night, in a Vietnamese restaurant, behind a paper screen, she tells you about her first husband, Dirk. Dirk comes home drunk one night—2:30 in the morning—and chases her out of their bed, out the back door, past the blackberry bushes and around the outside of the house trying to have sex with her. "I know my rights!" he shouts as he chases. He is running with a hard-on, Becky says. "I know my rights!" he calls out. It's easy to get away from him because he's drunk. Eventually Dirk falls down on the grass and goes to sleep right there. It is not long after that, Becky says, that she leaves him.

Becky is married now to a man named William, a soft-spoken gentle man. You wonder if William has anger in him; you've never seen a sign of it. You wonder if William knows the story of Dirk shouting, "I know my rights!" It's a story that causes you and Becky to collapse in laughter whenever either of you mentions it, though you both know that the story isn't really funny.

You have one more night at the lodge. You've read a book every day and you feel as if you've walked hundreds of miles. You've sat motionless on the dock and watched small dark fish, lurking in the weeds. Every evening, from your room, you listen for the loons.

You phone Alex. You talk to him and Zoe and tell them you'll be home after lunch the next day. Alex says he's glad you're ready to come back. Zoe tells you a new boy has joined her French class, even though it's nearly the end of the school year. The girls chase him during morning break and try to tag him. She does not, she says, because she thinks they're silly.

You hang up the receiver and think about all the parts of your life. You tell yourself that you have to believe they come together to make one life, your life. The one you live every day. You insist that this is possible, that all the parts of your life can add up to one.

Special meal tonight. Most of the guests will be leaving tomorrow, end of the week. There is an air of excitement in the dining-room. Bert's cheeks are flushed; he seems outraged as you enter. You are going to escape, having provided no explanation to HIM.

"Here she is!" he yells to his wife. "Why she would come to a place like this alone is beyond me." You stare eye-to-eye, from the annex window. Is there something you should do? Something you should say?

Bert is rising from his chair. He has finally worked himself up to some action. "I'll find out about her," he tells the others at his table. He stumps across the room, stands ten paces back, opens his mouth to shout.

You touch your ears, you touch your lips. Are you deaf? Are you mute? Are you neither of these? You smile as you turn away. Your head is framed by the open window.

A Gift of Forty

It was Marge's birthday and she drove, in the afternoon, to see her mother and father. She knew this was a time in her parents' lives when even a short visit from her would be drawn in deep, turned and examined, detail upon detail, for days and weeks to follow. The certain knowledge of this made Marge uneasy, even raising twinges—but she had sworn to herself years before that she would assume no more guilt on their behalf.

"Your father is with the dog," her mother said as she opened the door, and Marge knew she was glad to have been found in alone. "He goes farther every day. Hours sometimes. At his age. I don't even know where they walk. Not that I care," she added. She sat in the kitchen and her hands rested on the table, clasped as if poised for an event.

"You should get out more yourself, Ma. How long since you've taken a good walk in the fresh air?"

"Who needs it?" her mother said. "Anyway, it's windy today, and the wind gives me earache. If he needs it, let him take the walk. But not me. I dust, I read, I wipe the floor with a damp mop—sometimes on my knees—that's my exercise." She gestured and settled back as if awaiting Marge's contribution.

"It's my birthday. Did you remember?" Marge said, teasing a little.

"I knew." She turned to look out the window. "There's a small package in the middle drawer of the buffet. I didn't go out to get a card. I put it in Christmas paper."

"I'll see it later," Marge said, and didn't care, one way or another.

"It's a long time, 40 years."

"I don't feel so old," Marge said.

"I feel old thinking about it."

Her mother straightened her dress as she stood to make the tea. She pulled back the curtain to look down the street.

"He won't be back for a long time; we can talk in peace. He never hears a word when we're alone but when we've got company, he interrupts even from the basement."

"I'm not company, Ma." Marge opened the cupboard she knew, and took out the cups, the saucers. "I'm not company. And I like to see *him*, too."

"We don't talk the same when he's here, is all," her mother said. "He and I hardly speak when we're alone. *Do you want meat for supper? Is the celery hard to chew? The mail is here.*" She sat at the table again. "If he had a son, he could talk to his son in his old age. I talk to my daughter."

"You shouldn't split things down the middle like that, Ma. He's my father and I love him the same as I love you."

"What *you* know!" her mother said.

"What's the matter today? I drove here two hours. Let's go to a restaurant for tea, something different. I think you should get out."

"I'm going to tell a story," her mother said. "One you better know. I can tell it here, while we have tea."

"I don't want the story, Ma. Not if you're raking old dead leaves. We've gone through all this."

"Not this. I promised on my mother's Bible I would tell you when you're 40."

"Promised who?"

"Myself."

Her mother's tears took Marge by surprise.

"I wouldn't have come if I'd known you'd start to cry," Marge said. "What's so old and important it makes you cry? Me? It's my birthday—I'm 40—so what. In a minute you'll have *me* feeling bad."

"When you were born," she said, "when you were a brand new baby...just a minute."

She left the room and went down the hall. Marge heard her blow her nose, the taps running.

She came back.

"When you were a brand new baby," she started again, "I had to swear to something. But I never lived with it since."

Marge watched her mother and wondered at herself becoming afraid. They both knew about troubles. Marge had troubles. These she did not discuss. But something about her mother was making her afraid. Her mother's face had clenched; her hands, her knuckles were streaked white.

"It's not so easy," she said, and started again. "When you were born, there were certain things in the family...events that caused," and she paused, "...grief."

She looked so helpless having started this, Marge could have scooped her up with her two arms.

"Ma, this isn't any good...it isn't necessary. Whatever it is doesn't matter anymore. What difference will it make? Forty years is forty years and nothing changes that. Do you think I care what it is?"

"I do," her mother said, and glared hard out the window.

"I was made pregnant," she said, "by a boy who worked on the line with me in the glass factory. His name was Hawks. His parents—we had to tell them—mine, too—were so upset you'd have thought I'd laid down a snare. I didn't even know it was making a baby when it happened," she said. "I felt him fumbling around down there—it's a fact," she said. "You must think I was pretty stupid. And I was. It happened in the platform swing at my parents, out the back. The porch light was off. It was the only time but we weren't lucky. Kissing, I knew, but not about the other. It scared me, what he was doing, but I thought he must know what was what.

"His parents came to the house—Hawks wasn't with them—and said he couldn't marry me. He'd been sent to an uncle in the east. They wanted to fix things another way.

"There was a man, they told my parents, a good man, but older...his wife died suddenly of aneurysm in the head...in the brain, you know. He had no children and he was lonely. He lived 60 miles away. They knew him because of he'd been a friend to Hawks' father. They'd already talked it over. The whole plan was made. He would marry me, right after I had the baby, not before—he couldn't do that, he said—but he would take the baby too and move us to his place. Here," she said. Her palms opened to show the kitchen, the house. "Nobody asked if he wanted to meet me first and nobody asked if I wanted to marry him. My parents said it was the best thing."

"But my father?" Marge said.

"Not."

The two women stared, like strangers.

"My part—they made it a big deal, and it *was* in those days, because what could a pregnant girl do after? My part was, I had to swear when you were born, never to tell about the real father. Hawks had left; he stayed in the east and had his life. I know he married, had one baby girl. Nell, my friend, she found out, and wrote to tell me."

"A sister, Ma?"

"Who knows now? Nell wouldn't have lied to me then. I heard once from Hawks but that was right after they sent him away. You see, I wasn't supposed to mess up *his* life. And if he were to marry, his wife was never to be told. That was the arrangement. For finding me a husband." She snorted.

"You should have told me, Ma." Marge was rocking back and forth, looking down at the floor.

"Lots of times I wanted to tell. But I was the only one. Everyone said, let it lie, you gave your word. But I'm the one couldn't live with it. Now they're all dead. My parents, his parents. I don't know about Hawks. Who cares about his wife and what they made me say 40 years ago."

"You should have told me, Ma."

They heard the dog dragging his chain outside, and footsteps after him. The dog scratched and whined at the door.

"In the buffet," her mother spoke quickly, "in the middle drawer, you'll see the Christmas wrap. It's a photo, the only one. Hawks was nineteen. It was with the letter. If he sent any other, I never got it. The letter said three sentences: *My uncle swallows a big spoon of butter after every meal. It makes me sick. I didn't want to come here.* That, and the photo."

The old man, out of breath, opened the side door. He was smiling because he'd seen Marge's car. His eyes were watery and his cap was puffed up like a baker's, from the wind. The dog bounded toward Marge and the sight of the two of them coming to greet her made the women weep, the mother for what she had to tell, the daughter for what she had to hear.

76

Graveyard Shift

On the way home from work, Judith surprised herself by
pulling off the main road and driving through the gates of the
cemetery. She crossed the old part of the graveyard and took
the short-cut, a dirt road that followed the cliff and led to a
lower meadow. A new section had been opened to make space
for the "newly dead." Her father was one of the newly dead. If
newly could mean almost a year.

Someone had told her, during the two years she and Tosh
had lived in the Black Forest—he'd taught Linguistics at

Freiburg while she completed research for her graduate degree in Nursing—that the Germans buried their dead in vertical position, upright. Better use of space. After so many years, perhaps generations, they were dug up. What happened then? Cremation, probably. Cremains. "New word coming into the dictionary," Tosh had said. It was the word used by the cemetery director when she and Eddie had come to make *arrangements* for their father. "I'll look after the arrangements," the director had said, as if their father had been a loose bunch of dried flowers. "It's my job to make things easier for you." He looked pleased with himself, saying this.

During the fifties, on an occasional weekend, their father borrowed a car—he never owned one of his own during those early family years—and took Judith and Eddie and their mother out for a drive. That's what people did in the fifties: went for drives in the country on Sunday afternoons. Saturdays at their house were kept for buying groceries and cleaning the icebox; later, for defrosting the fridge. During those Sunday rambles, every time their father drove past a cemetery, he'd call out, long after the question was old and stale, "How many people are dead in *this* graveyard?" She or Eddie would shout back, just to complete the joke: "All of them." Yuk yuk.

Cremains. The director was fawning and attentive; Judith hated him instantly. "If your father's wishes were that he be cremated," he said, "the cremains must be laid to rest in Memory Garden, not in the main cemetery." The director wore expensive clothes, expensive jewellery; Judith spied gold chains beneath the shirt collar. Memory Garden, he explained with practised patience, was an enclosure within an enclosure, kept separate by circumscribing knee-high walls. He led Judith and Eddie out of his tasteful graveyard office, which had grave sorts of displays down one wall, and drove them in a black limousine, not a hearse, past tombstones and mausolea, past war-graves, past what he called "the Chinese section," past graves of the famous, through narrow roads, twisting and turning, until finally, they descended the cliff. In Memory Garden, there were no tombstones, only flat lozenges as long as Judith's foot.

"Father would hate this," Judith told Eddie, as soon as she could pull him off one of the footpaths and away from the director. "This guy's greet-the-mourners routine is so perfect I can't stand it. He keeps talking about lining the earth with plastic grass so no-one will be offended. Who's going to be offended by dirt? Are you? Is Mother? I'd like to throw a handful of it. At him." Judith knew she might begin to cry. If she started, she might never stop.

Eddie refused to answer. The director had become wary, dealing face-to-face with Judith. Eddie chose a number from a chart, a tiny double plot, knowing their mother would not or could not make the decision. Judith threatened to tear the artificial grass out of the hole before their father's ashes were put in. She refused to say cremains.

"Please," said Eddie the peacemaker. "Please."

Eddie had phoned from the West Coast after their father's second heart attack; their mother, who'd been manic-depressive for the past seven years, had just been admitted in the manic state to the same hospital where their father lay dying and where Judith worked as a nurse. Each was in a different wing—their mother in Psychiatry—but Judith was the only one of the three who could come and go.

"I'm so sorry," Eddie said. "I can't tell you how sorry I am." Meaning that Judith was the one who lived here, the one who had to deal with it, *it* being a loaded word representing daily confusions, entanglements, sufferings. Judith sometimes saw herself as manager of the family's lunacies and grief. She did not tell Eddie that this time, their mother had removed her clothes in the car on the way to hospital and created such a disturbance, three policemen were called, one of whom she strong-armed as he tried to drag her out of the car. When they finally carried her, naked, outstretched and shouting, into Emergency, she suddenly became quiet and with a meek and gentle smile told the doctor on duty she'd ram an umbrella up his arse and open it, as soon as she got the chance. After he'd sedated her and just before the drug began to take effect, she looked at him slyly and said, "I know what *you'd* look like from behind in your altogether. You'd have a piggy-bum." Their mother recovered—to both propriety and a depressive state. Their father did not.

The day after her admission, Judith's mother looked at her across the bed-rails. Judith had just finished the graveyard shift—what Tosh called the grave-watch—and had stopped in to say goodbye before she went home to crawl into bed beside Tosh, just before he'd have to get up to go to work himself. "Aren't we a pair," her mother said. "Your father and I. Falling apart at the same time. We're just going to have to wing it, dear. We'll just have to wing it."

A wing and a prayer. Where did that come from? Tosh would be sure to know.

"It's Looney Tunes," Judith had told Eddie, on the phone. "Looney Tunes. By the time you get here, we'll all be nuts."

Judith and Eddie expected a fight from the director about the memorial marker for their father's grave. Eddie had agreed to look after that, but before the funeral he insisted on a separate trip to the office, alone. Father's instructions had been explicit; he wanted his name, date of birth, date of death, and an inscription on the third line: *Life's Work Incomplete.* The details of what their father had not completed were not known to Judith and Eddie. Or to their mother, for that matter. She smiled sweetly from her rolled-up hospital bed as Eddie read out their father's wishes. (Drugged, Judith thought, recognizing the signs. She's drugged.) "Your father was eccentric," their mother said. Then, she pulled herself forward and a voice that had dropped almost an octave, clearly said: "You see how connected we are, to our dead."

Judith looked quickly but her mother had already drifted back against the pillow. Her expression, oddly enough, was similar to one Judith had become used to on the Neuro ward. Patients, not realizing what was happening, came up to Judith sometimes with that secretive, dreamy look—just before they had a convulsion. "Nurse," they'd say, "Oh, Nurse." But there would be confusion. She'd learned to get them on the floor quickly, or into their beds with the padded sides up—if there was time.

The director's objections had been surprisingly mild. Perhaps he was mindful of Judith's threat to tear out the plastic grass. Judith found out from Eddie, later, what he'd said. "Think of taste," he told Eddie. "In a year or two you and your sister might be sorry you didn't choose *R-I-P* or *In Loving Memory* as our other Garden families do. Your mother will rest beside him some day. What will she think?" (I'd love to invite you to ask, Judith thought, when she heard this.) "I only warn you to consider future costs to yourselves," the director went on. "You may be sorry if you change your minds." Eddie and Judith had not changed their minds.

And while the two of them, the director, Tosh, Eddie's wife Frances, and the minister, stood for a private service in the midst of Memory Garden, their mother, ten blocks away, had stood at the end of her bed and thrown a four-pound ashtray through her hospital-room wall.

What would their father have said if he could have seen himself in a little brown box under Eddie's arm—his box about to be nestled by shredded plastic? Judith had wondered, between her teeth, if the ashes that Eddie had been handed to place in the hole were really their father's. "How do we know they're all there?" Eddie had said, "Please, Judith, don't rip out the plastic grass; don't argue about the ashes, please please please." He'd looked so anxious and worried, she'd promised not to do either.

Tosh had remained silent. So had Frances; she'd flown in from BC for a day and a night, just for the funeral. And grave-yard workers, in sombre-coloured work-clothes, huddled near the base of the cliff by a clump of trees, waiting for the service to be over so they could get back to work.

Later, they visited their mother. The hole in the wall gaped above her as she lay, very still, in her hospital bed.

For months after the cremation and funeral, Judith wondered about her father's teardrop shape; she was sorry they would never have a chance to find it. Tosh had told her about this, years ago; it was part of his Japanese mythology. After a body was cremated, the family, the survivors, raked through the hot ashes and plucked out the teardrop shape. It was kept, saved; Judith no longer remembered where. Did it contain the essence, the soul? Was it bone? "What if it can't be found? What if there isn't one? What if it's not there?" she'd asked, putting up arguments. "What if it isn't the right shape?"

Tosh's face had been maddeningly confident. "If you look long enough...it will be there."

That same face she never tired of watching when Tosh was asleep. That wore the patience of his ancestors, she teased. That she never tired of running her fingers over. The carved mask of the wide high cheekbones. The same face that (long before she'd been part of his life) had been expertly trained to conceal its own pain.

Judith and Tosh had eloped—a minor or major contribution to *Life's Work Incomplete*. How was her father to deal with that? Nothing during a lifetime within the boundaries of Ontario had prepared him for the phone call at Christmas from his only daughter, then travelling in Madrid, saying she'd married Tosh, a Canadian. Japanese-Canadian, she'd added. Her father had never met a Japanese. Nor a Japanese-Canadian. For that matter, he'd never met anyone from Madrid, though had she brought home a Spaniard, that, Judith knew, would have been acceptable. Theirs was a family of secrets hidden for generations, grudges held a lifetime. Twelve years after her marriage, Judith learned what happened at her parents' home the night she phoned. To her surprise, it was Frances, Eddie's wife, who gave up the information. In Judith's home. The night they buried their father's ashes. Frances, who'd always given the impression of being capable of remaining outside, even above, the precarious trapdoors and vicissitudes of Eddie's family.

Eddie and Frances were staying with Judith and Tosh. After the funeral and the visit to hospital, the four had gone back to the house, made sandwiches, opened a bottle of wine. Frances was to fly out in the morning; Eddie would stay one more week to help Judith. During the next few days they would sort through their father's papers—a job neither looked forward to.

Judith wasn't sure how they got onto the topic but she'd always known that Eddie had been home for Christmas the year she'd phoned to say that she and Tosh had eloped.

"What did he say, Eddie? You were there. He must have said something."

Eddie was the peacemaker. A peacemaker did not stir up trouble in the family.

"What's the point?" he said. "Why now?"

"Because I need to know. Especially now."

"To satisfy your curiosity?"

"Isn't that enough? You know something about me that I'd like to know. That isn't fair. I need to settle things; I have to understand."

Judith had always been accused, within the family, of digging at her life with a backward pick. The fact that her life was intertangled with theirs was an irritant the others had learned to tolerate—the way they would a recurring bad dream.

"I know," said Frances. "I was there."

The other three stared at her.

"Frances," said Eddie, "there's no point."

83

"Quiet, Eddie." Judith turned to Frances. "You were there when I called? You were there in my parents' home? I didn't know that."

"We were both there. It was Christmas, remember? It was the year before Eddie and I were married. Everyone thought you were coming home after your trip to Spain."

"I did come home...and brought Tosh."

"Not until five days later. I'd left by then. But I was there when you called."

Throughout this, Tosh's face had not altered. He was amused; Judith had learned the signs, albeit with difficulty. And Tosh and her father had become friends, years ago.

"What he said was: 'We fought a war against the goddam Japs.' " Frances gulped at her wine.

"What? Who? Father said that? He did?"

"He did," said Frances. "That's all he said. Then, he went to bed. He went to bed and pulled the covers over his head. For three days."

Judith found herself giggling and giggling. She couldn't stop. Eddie started laughing, too. What else was there to tell? Nothing, it seemed. The rest, Judith knew. Or thought she knew.

She and Tosh had taken a taxi from the airport. Were driven through streets that crackled with cold. Judith felt she had *done* something to her parents. Given them a Japanese son-in-law who had to be both imagined and admitted to the family in the same instant. She and Tosh gripped hands in the back seat; arrived outside her parents' home. Expected, but the porch light was off. The porch was used only in summer; a second front door with a window in its upper half led to the living-room. The outer door was unlocked so they went into the porch and began to take off their boots. As Judith leaned forward to tug at hers, the curtain on the living-room door was swept aside, and through the window she saw the face of her father. She and Tosh were in the dark but her father was illuminated from behind. His face looked unnatural to Judith. Knotted. Disfigured, somehow. As if he were clutched in some grimace he could not let go. His skin was white, his mouth open. *Corpse*, Judith thought. *Daddy looks like a corpse.* Later, in retrospect, she did not recall thinking that her behaviour might have killed him. At the time, she'd thought only: *Daddy looks like a corpse.*

The door was whipped open; her father stumbled forward with one hand outstretched. Before Judith could speak or introduce, Tosh had gripped her father's hand and said loudly and clearly: "Hi Dad."

Oh yes, young as they both were, Judith knew then and for all time how Tosh had learned the power of the word.

Judith left her car and walked along the path to Memory Garden. Walked between rows of flat markers, each hiding its urn or box beneath. Each lozenge concealed its own teardrop shape. Perhaps it was good that the one belonging to her father had never been looked for. Tosh's mythology had never quite explained what one did with it, once it was found. And there it was, in its row, the tiny plot that contained a blank tablet for her mother and beside that, *Life's Work Incomplete.*

Judith tried to conjure her father, the sort of man he'd been. A man of his generation—of the Depression and of the Second Great War. Who'd lived a life he'd considered and described as incomplete. Had he lived longer, Judith doubted that he'd have altered the inscription. He was a man who worked in the aircraft industry during the war. Who borrowed a car in the fifties and took his family for Sunday drives. Who told his children stories he invented at the moment of the telling. Who used a cross-cut saw to cut wood for the stove, who played horseshoes with his neighbour, who sat his children on a chair and told them to stay put until they'd learned to tie their laces. Who was perplexed and defeated by his wife's implacable descent to the world of the mentally ill. And who'd never met anyone Japanese, until Tosh. Tosh, whose own childhood had been devoured in BC in a prisoner-of-war camp that the Canadian Japanese were themselves forced to erect. Tosh, whose ancestors had been in this country longer than her father's own.

Judith and Eddie did not enjoy going through the papers after their father's death. It was a dreary and depressing task made moreso by their mother's drug-induced lethargy when they visited her each evening on the ward.

What they found was what they expected: insurance policies, bank books, bills paid, tax files up-to-date.

Except for one surprise. A letter, which Judith had never seen. Neither she nor Eddie had known of its existence. It revealed itself the way an unexpected but entirely appropriate event in a novel is exposed and around which subsequent important details turn. But in Judith's story, the details were important to no-one but her.

The letter was typed but undated; clearly, from its content, it had been sent at the beginning of 1942. The same year three-year-old Tosh had been marched off to the mountains to live in a chicken coop throughout the BC winter. The letter was still in its envelope, stamped with the lion and the unicorn and was from the Office of the Prime Minister. It was addressed to her father:

> The Japanese attack on the territories of the United States and the British Commonwealth has served to bring the international gangsters out in the open as one. Now, with war on all continents, there is a greater need than ever for aircraft, and for all the other machines and munitions of war. President Roosevelt has told the workers of the United States, as Prime Minister Churchill has told the workers of Britain, that for the next few months there is...an all important gap to fill.

...there can be no finer motto for the new year than..."Brave men shall not die because I have faltered." Nowhere could it possibly be of greater significance than in aircraft production. You will, I am sure, make it yours for 1942.

Yours sincerely
W.L. Mackenzie King

Their father had never discussed the war. Perhaps this had something to do with him not going to war. He had never mentioned the letter. Judith tried to imagine him inside an aircraft plant. Had he been on an assembly line, shaping parts for planes destined for battle? The image of her father in his youth, shirt-sleeves rolled up, became confused with an image of Tosh as international gangster. Enemy alien. Gangster or alien? Had the letter from the Prime Minister helped to make them one and the same for her father? White, mattered. Shape of eyes, mattered. Skin, mattered. Especially in Ontario. Certainly in BC.

She thought of something Tosh had read to her this week from the morning paper. It concerned the new morgue, recently opened. "Two different worlds," said the article, comparing the new morgue with the old.

Two different worlds. At the time, the news item had broken her up. To break up. To break down. Life's fine lines. The night of the funeral, after they'd finished the wine, Frances had asked: "If you and Tosh decide to have a child, what could that child present *you* with...that would be unthinkable?"

Something Judith could not yet, or ever—because that was the way of surprises—imagine.

Judith had brought no flower to the grave. She could think of no word powerful enough to say. She thought only, as she looked down at the marker, *Oh Father, this is what we come to. We are what we are. We do what we can.*

She left Memory Garden, again taking the short-cut up the cliff road. The dirt road permitted the width of only one vehicle and as she rounded the curve, she was forced to stop because another car blocked the way. A blue car, parked on a slant, pointing uphill.

A man was outside the car on the driver's side, the trousers of what appeared to be an expensive suit bunched around his ankles. His buttocks were rising and falling in the sun. A woman's legs were sticking out through the open doorway. The man was so startled when he realized Judith's car was behind him, he jerked back, looked at Judith—his face perplexed? stricken?—and abandoning the woman, began to run up the hill. The woman's legs were left dangling. The man was still wearing his suit jacket and did not stop to pull up his trousers. Judith sat in her car (these moments unfolding quickly; she and he shocked and amazed) and she watched his bum, pale even in the sun, his creases of fat wrinkling as he ran.

Although this had not been Judith's first response, she now began to laugh and laugh as she saw that the man's bum looked exactly like what her mother would describe as a piggy-bum. By this time the man had run almost to the top of the hill. (Judith—the nurse Judith—asked herself: Is he in shock?) Still running, he was belatedly trying to yank up his pants.

Judith backed her car down the cliff road, thinking of the last line of a childhood story her father had once invented and which had left her and Eddie disgruntled because of the lack of resolution: "For all I know, he may be running still."

She took the long route back, stopped the car outside the director's office and went inside. She was greeted by the same face, the same gold chains beneath the shirt. She knew that the director recognized her, even after a year.

"There are two people fucking in a blue car," she told him. "On the cliff road just above my father's grave. Above Memory Garden."

She knew by his face, as she left—he had not spoken one word—that he had been offended. Not by her news, but by her language. The power of one word. The pretence that it was not in his repertoire. Indeed, his face had received the word with remorse, as if *she'd* been the one who'd committed an act of very bad taste.

Her father had been an ordinary man trying to live an ordinary life. But lives became intertangled, confused; events led people awry. Her patients. Different worlds. Her mother—still on medication—between worlds. Manic states and startled faces and piggy-bums. Judith's life and Tosh's. International gangsters, enemy aliens, letters from the Prime Minister. Legs dangling out of cars. This was life. Life at this moment. While she was passing through the cemetery gates, rejoining traffic on the main road.

Man Without Face

There is a man in one of my old childhood comics and in the story, the man has stopped overnight at a hotel in an English town. One of those towns with narrow red-brick houses and unfriendly ruddy-cheeked citizens; a town where men wear tweeds and black scapulars as they stride over cobbled streets.

In the morning, when the man goes to the sink to wash and shave he looks in the mirror, but *he has no face*. Where eyes eyebrows nose and mouth had been, there is only an oval of smooth blank skin. Did his face rub off on the towel? Did I then ask myself: how can he see his no-face if he has no eyes?

How can he breathe with no nose, no mouth? By some leap of faith into true horror, the man at the sink and I knew and believed that all of this was possible.

Why do I think of this, why, when I think of my own father tripping off my front step and falling flat on *his* face on the newcut grass? Always one to cover his tracks, he picked himself up and stepped, even nimbly, into the waiting taxi. No more was said about it. Perhaps, at the hotel the next morning, he didn't remember. That's the part I never knew and never asked. How much did he remember?

Just before Father fell on his face, he'd been sitting on my living-room rug trying to organize a sing-song. He was wearing a summer shirt and khaki shorts. His cheeks were flushed and he was slapping his bare legs against the rug as he roared through the lyrics of "In the Summertime," a song he knew well but that none of us did. Not that we could have sung with him anyway. Not I, nor my husband, nor our children, nor my twin sister Beryl, who lived in the same city. Not one of us sang with my father.

Every summer, when Beryl—whom I'd nicknamed Burr— and I were children, father tumbled out of his lawnchair and fractured ribs. After the first fall, he allowed mother to put him in a taxi and have him driven to the office of Dr. Partridge who told him he was lucky he had neither internal bleeding nor punctured lung. He was told to stop drinking and to buy himself an elasticized girdle for support. Father told mother to buy him a woman's high-fitting girdle and after that, every summer, he prescribed his own treatment and strapped his own ribs. He would not go back to that old bird Partridge, he said; he'd no intention of listening to another lecture on the hazards of life.

Burr and I lived with our parents a mile and a half from Greenly. We had no family car, so to do our shopping we had to take a bus that rattled past our house on the dirt road. There

91

was little traffic but occasionally, some old car bumped by and raised a cloud of dust and Father would say, "There goes Percy to take salt to his cows," or "Mrs. Leary must have run off on Telly again. Serves him right, the damned fool."

Behind the house and beyond a fold of hills, there was a rocky place thick with trees. A ten-minute walk past that took us to a waterfall that cut its way down a narrow gorge and opened to slow rolling farmland. The place we lived in was not like that. Thorn and crabapple and chokecherry grew close together and dust blew in off the road. That's how I remember it, anyway.

Burr and I made our way as often as we could to the waterfall. The climb was steep but midway to the top and behind the water, there was a kind of half-cave, a niche where we could hide away without getting wet, where we could bring our comics to read, where we could watch the watertumble down—and discuss our father. His drinking was the first topic before we got to the second: why did Mother marry him?

"Why does he drink?"

"How should I know?"

"Do you think he's always been like this?"

"If he has, why would she have married him?"

"Why did they have *us*?"

We broke off pieces of limestone from the sides of the cave and tossed them through the waterfall. If Father had known where we were, we'd have been in trouble.

"The old fart," Burr said, daring, watching to see if I'd react.

"Old fart," I said back, and threw a chunk of stone.

"Old fart, old fart." We chanted into the back of the waterfall, louder and louder, until we were shouting above its roar, holding our sides, amazed at the release of our own laughter.

We became serious again.

"What about Mother? Why does she put up with him?"

"She's trying to keep the peace."

This was an expression our mother herself used. In tight-lipped grimace she said, "Try to keep the peace," as she fed us

92

early on a Friday night before he came home from the tavern where he'd already begun his weekend binge after leaving the cheese factory. Dressed in his old suit, shirt and tie, he'd just performed his week's work, keeping the books in a tiny office that reeked of curds.

Mother invented errands, sent us outside. Never, as far as we could see, tried to alter his behaviour. No, that's not true. There were a few rare times when Burr and I were witness to whole bottles of whisky being poured down the sink, a prelude to Mother fighting him for all she was worth.

Behind the waterfall we tried to understand what we had done that had landed the two of us into a family as godforsaken as ours. We thought we were born realists, something we'd heard Mother call herself. If we had to take after someone, we said, it wasn't going to be him. It never occurred to us in any realistic way that there might be any other sort of father. He was the one we had.

"Why do they fight?"

"Maybe they hate each other."

"They got married, didn't they?"

"Maybe he didn't drink then."

"Maybe he started drinking after they had *us*."

One time, we went home and sneaked into a silent house and opened the glass door of the china cabinet. We lifted out the charcoal-covered prayer book and searched for the passage we wanted and laid the book on the dining-room table. A frayed silken cord kept the pages open at the marriage vows. But the book silently found its way back to the shelf behind glass before we were up the next morning, and we did not know who had replaced it. This disappointed us because we wanted the two of them to know that we were part of this, too; that we had to shift and bend with every ripple the two of them made.

The summer we were nine, the daily paper ran an article called: *Take this test to see if you're an alcoholic.* Burr and I cut out the article and administered the test—not to Father, but to each other. Behind the waterfall, we learned the questions by heart: *Have you begun to invent excuses for having a drink? Do you try to push drinks onto others?* No, no, we answered. *Do you drink to forget your troubles?* And the most ominous of all: *Do you drink alone?*

After we'd given the test to each other, we answered for Father. Three truthful yes answers meant a drinking problem. But unlike the marriage vows in the prayer book, we did not leave the newspaper test lying around on the dining-room table. We couldn't go *that far.* Because Father's drinking, except between Burr and me, was never discussed.

There was always the next day. The real morning after. When living people rose from their beds and had breakfast and stayed in or went out—to school, to work, to play—and carried on with their lives. Even born realists who lived together and looked one another in the eye and spoke the way they believed other people spoke. But did not mention, no, never mentioned the night before, the day before, the weekend of stumbling, of spilling, of drunken singing, of maudlin tears. Never mentioned Father falling into the empty tub and, arm outstretched, halfway through the bathroom wall; never mentioned the broken glass, the stains on the rug, the holes in the plaster, the lawnchair collapses, the slips on the ice, the broken ribs, ankles, bones. The weeping red-rimmed eyes.

How could we get up in the morning and never mention any of this?

Because these were our real lives.

Because Father got out of bed Monday morning, put on his old suit, stood on the dirt road to be picked up by the factory truck—and went back to work. In some wild and implausible way, he convinced us that he could function. And Burr and I returned to school; pushed down the fear that had knotted in our stomachs like a lurking tiger, since Friday afternoon.

Christmas: Burr and I are ten years old. Father lifts the tree with one hand. He storms through the living-room, out the

94

front door—bulbs attached, cords frayed and flying—and plants the tree in the snowbank.

Who brought it back inside? Rescued the surviving bulbs, the frosty angels? Who went down on hand and knee to shake the snow from bruised needles and limbs?

Christmas: Burr and I are eleven. Father sits in his green chair in the living-room and, Christmas Eve, begins a slow and steady binge that will last until New Year's Day. He holds his glass in a salute to anyone who walks through the room, and sings:

Hither, page, and stand by me,
If thou knows't it telling,
Yonder peasant, who is he?
Where and what his dwelling?

He tries to whip up speed in the lyrics but his tongue thickens and he's lodged in his chair and only one arm is able to beat itself against the upholstery.

The last three days he carries his whisky to his room and stays there. Mother comes down to the living-room to sleep on the couch. On New Year's Day, he emerges. Showers, shaves and comes into the living-room, whistling. It's as if he's been away on a slightly wearing trip. He reaches under the tree and pulls out our gift, the one he's refused at Christmas. It's a photograph of Burr and me, taken at Woolworth's in Greenly, and framed by ourselves. He rolls his eyes toward the ceiling as if to a distant agreeing oracle and says, in a way that only he seems to understand: "By their fruits ye shall know them," which drives Burr and me back to the cave, despite the icicles and the slippery climb.

"Do you think we're like him? That we'll turn out like him?"

"We'll leave before that can happen," says Burr.

Where was Mother during this time?

She was keeping the peace.

There were acts of Mother's that we admired. Her capacity to avoid argument. Her ability to feign sleep; so practised was she at this she was able to fool Burr and me some of the time. We admired her resolution. Four days a week she took the bus to Sadie's Dress Shop on Greenly's Main Street where, from the day Burr and I began school, she was head seamstress. Mother, in fact, had a narrowly circumscribed life of her own. She had a small income; she had a few friends who, like herself, worked at the shop and with whom she went out occasionally but whom she never invited home. This, Burr and I understood: our own best friends were more or less kept in hiding over a period of fifteen years.

Long after Burr and I left home, we phoned each other, going over and over the same ground. By then, we were married and had children of our own. But we talked as if there was still something we could do about Father's drinking: acknowledge it, make it public, somehow. To free Mother, we said. To free ourselves. "The patterns are entrenched," we said, into the phone. "Thank God we got out. But how can she put up with him? How *can* she have stayed with him all these years?"

"Too late to leave," said Burr. "Neither of them can make a move now."

We sent each other identical newspaper clippings: *Nine out of ten wives stay with alcoholic husbands. One husband in ten will stay with an alcoholic wife.*

Once, we went into hysterics when Burr, having put her children to bed a few minutes earlier, told me she'd just poured herself a sherry.

"*Do you drink alone?*" I said, in my behind the waterfall voice.

We continued to make the climb in good weather, even after our bodies had grown too large to fit the cave. During our early teens we sat on the ground at the bottom of the falls and scratched boys' initials onto flat layers of rock. We knew we were too far from home to be found; in any case, there was no-one to come looking. Mother was at the shop until five; Father at the cheese factory until six when the truck dropped him off.

Some days he brought home a block of cheese that he stored in the root cellar, the entrance of which was a double trapdoor around one side of the house. Burr and I seldom lifted those wooden slats; a few times, while Father was at work, we did so on a dare, and descended the wooden ladder. Once down in that stifling space we had to hunch shoulders and bow our heads. Father had run a wire through the floor of the house and hooked up a swinging socket but this rarely contained a bulb. Burr and I encouraged each other to hold our breath so we wouldn't have to inhale the underground. I believed the place was alive. Burr called it the rat-cellar instead of the root cellar.

While we were there we inspected Father's whisky, for this is where he kept his stash. He'd banged shelves into an earth wall...one shelf held ageing blocks of cheese; surprisingly, there was little dampness in that room underground. Another shelf held his whisky—five or six bottles at a time. Never fewer than three. The store, he called it. Go down and see what I've got in the store. And Burr and I, even though we might know, would hold our breath, and go down.

Father walks through the back door each evening and reaches for the bottle he's brought up the night before. He's taken to announcing in a loud voice, "The bar is officially open," as if granting himself licence. As if this is a safe joke, an opening line to which there is no reply.

How does he know we won't speak? That we won't scream, throw plates, dump whisky down the drain. That we won't cry or despair or quietly plead, "Please go somewhere and get help. You have a drinking problem."

How can he count on our silence?

This is the part that is most difficult to understand.

Father has to take only two drinks now, before he starts to weave his way across the room. "I can hold my liquor," he says, but doesn't look us in the eye. "Don't ever think I can't hold my liquor."

We hear him from the green chair:

O mother, O mother, make my bed
Make it both long and narrow

then, silence. We don't need to see his face to know that he's begun to weep, as he often does, now.

"Think of his face," I said to Burr one day, when I was sitting in the kitchen of her apartment.

Burr looked over, saw me as I saw her, saw the cold stone that lay at the bottom of our lives.

"Flushed," she said. "Moist eyes." She sat down.

"Moist around the lips," I said. "Soft chin. And wrinkles...from the corners of his mouth up across the cheeks."

"Extra folds of cheek," said Burr.

"A wonder, really." We knew plenty of statistics. "He should be emaciated, malnourished."

"Mother keeps feeding him, meat and potatoes."

"What's she supposed to do? Let him starve?"

"Maybe," said Burr. "I mean, think of his liver."

We giggled dangerously, as if Father were in the next room. And then found ourselves doubled over.

Burr stood up, held onto her chair, addressed an unknown audience. "If you wonder why we laugh," she said, "if you'd spent the first fifteen years of your life edging away from tears, you'd laugh, too."

She sat down. We stopped laughing but continued to wipe our eyes. We were in a place we hadn't allowed ourselves for years. But the place still had no outlet, no escape.

"Enablers," I said. "That's what we're called now."

"The people who made up the word never had to look Father in the eye."

"Did *we*?"

Father has become tricky. We know this, but we never say it. It's something about his eyes, the red horizontal streaks through the whites, the narrowing of the focus, the pulling of the look into himself, fast, so we get just a flash, a quick hint of what he might do next. This is our cue to move sideways, exit, make a swift getaway. Sometimes I wonder if from above we look like a family of crabs, picking our way sideways to get around one another.

By now, he has bought a car, a second-hand Pontiac with a stick-shift behind the wheel. The car is two shades of green and breaks down a lot but Father manages to keep it going and no longer relies on the factory truck to travel back and forth to work.

During summer evenings and weekends, before *the bar is officially open*, he teaches me to drive on the dirt road. Burr and I are fifteen. Burr refuses to learn. I see it as a means of escape. She sees what's coming next.

And what's coming next is this: Father, on Friday nights after work, drives home and drops off the Pontiac before he heads now farther afield to do his drinking. He's picked up by the men he calls his drinking partners but tells us he's too smart to drive home with them. "They're all pie-eyed by nine o'clock," he says. "They can't hold their liquor worth a damn." But he, he wouldn't get behind the wheel after three drinks. To ensure that he gets home safely, he's decided that I will pick him up when he's ready to come home.

"Don't do it," says Burr, upstairs in our room. "I wouldn't. You'll only be helping him drink as much as he wants."

This is decades before the words *emotional blackmail* begin to appear in the articles we seek out and read.

Friday nights, Saturday nights, I don't know how long it goes on, Father phones when he is drunk and ready to come home, and I climb into the Pontiac and edge my way close to the shoulder of dirt roads and back highways, and collect him. I am always to wait in the car and this I do, watching for his swaying figure in doorways of hotels, houses, bars. A greenish sort of light shines across these openings; music blurts into the air with a suddenness that surprises; voices erupt and subside as if severed by the closing doors.

My father reaches out to steady himself against the passenger side. He slumps rather than slides in, and as soon as the door is shut he raises his head and begins a conversation as if it's normal for us to converse. Truth is, at home we hardly ever speak. The two of us are facing forward in the close whisky-breath space of the front seat and I can escape him no more than he can escape me. His slurred questions are barely understandable; they don't seem connected to my life or his. Sometimes, he foregoes the questions altogether and sings, instead:

Oh Susan MacGoozan'
The girl of my choosin'
She sticks to my bosom
like glue

One night, he reaches into his pocket and pulls out a handful of coins that he says are for me. When we get home he scatters them over the front seat. I wait until he goes to bed and I go out to scoop up the coins, wondering if he'll remember and take them back the next day.

Each time I get him home, I believe I have saved his life. It never occurs to me that if he is at the wheel he might kill someone else. I concentrate only on him and me: if he drives, he might die; if I drive, I keep him alive.

He is my father.

The summer we finish high school, a Saturday, Burr runs away. Father, who descends to the rat-cellar and comes up bearing a bottle, opens the bar early because it's the weekend. After two drinks and some prowling around he comes upon Burr's diary and reads portions of it aloud, making fun. Burr is furious. She will never forgive him, she says, never.

I know where she's gone, of course. Not far. There's only one place to go.

Father walks out to the road a couple of times, glass in hand, looks both ways, comes back to the yard and leans into the Pontiac.

"Where's your sister?" he says.

"I don't know."

"Where is she?"

"How should I know?"

He rolls his eyes and when he does this I'm reminded of the New Year's Day he surfaced to open the framed photograph of us, his children, his twins. *By their fruits ye shall know them.* I'm possessed of a rage I didn't know I contained, a rage I could not have let fly even moments before.

"It's your fault she ran away! It's your bloody fault!"

Me. Shouting at Father.

"What the hell are you talking about?"

His rage is greater than mine. His stance threatening. It stops me. Right there. The closest I've ever come: to naming it, naming him. I have a momentary insight into how Mother must feel. The reasons she leaves him alone. The incident closes over the way water closes over a mud-hole.

I sneak a chunk of ham and two apples out of the fridge and take them to the base of the waterfall. Burr comes out of hiding and I tell her that I've shouted at Father. I've come close to calling him—a drunk.

"But you didn't," she says, and her voice is flat. "Did you."

At the first sign of shadows in the fields, we walk home and go up to our room, unchallenged. Leggings over psoriasis: like every other encounter with Father this one is never mentioned. After we leave home, we say to each other. After we leave home if he so much as touches a drink in our presence, *we'll tell him.*

But after we leave home, nothing changes. Except that Burr and I move away. Mother stays; they go on living together as if there's no escape.

"He's coming here," I tell Burr. "They're both coming, for a visit. Only one night and they're staying at a hotel."

"So he can drink without censorship," she says, on the phone.

"Do you realize this is the first trip they've taken away from home?"

Burr and I have distanced ourselves, put a hundred and thirty miles between us and our childhood home. We can visit, but we can also get back to the city quickly. I think of the old dirt road, dust rolling in over the fields and settling on the long grass. Greenly has stretched out to the country now. It has surrounded and encompassed the waterfall—now a picnic site—and our parents' home, which is part of the town. I think of the cheese factory, shut down years ago. I think of Father's stash underground. Is it still there? Who buys the whisky? We know, of course, that Father doesn't drink the way he used to. Can't. Indirectly, Mother has let us know this as his health has become worse and worse. She does all the driving now. The bus service has stopped and the roads are paved. And she, too, has retired.

As Burr's apartment is small and located on the outskirts of the city, we decide that it will be easier to have the family meal at my home; Burr's family will stay overnight. "I'm not serving liquor," I say. "One bottle of wine for the adults, and that will have to be shared. He can't get drunk on that."

Father brings his own. A large bottle of cheap red wine, which he sets at his feet under the table. Before dinner, he pulls two miniature whisky bottles from his shirt pocket, and drinks the contents of those.

Burr and I are mute. The children chat with their grandmother and, after dinner, go out to play. Our husbands have heard our stories over and over again but they're not entangled the way we are, in our past. The patterns are concrete. No-one interferes with Father, who keeps us aloof and sinks into silence at his end of the table.

Until the momentary flush of rowdiness when he tries to

raise a sing-song after dinner, slapping his legs against the rug. Mother has already slipped quietly away and has driven herself back to the hotel. She kisses Burr and me at the door. "He'll come by taxi, later," she says. "I'll stop by for a few minutes on our way home in the morning. We can say good-bye then." And when Father leaves, not more than half-hour later, he falls flat on his face on my front lawn.

Burr and I lean against the door and curse and laugh in outrage and relief after the taxi pulls away. I swear to her that I'll say something the next day, not when he's drunk, when he's sober. I'll let him know, I'll let him know—no shouting or screaming—that it matters to us, that we're all in this together, that we, they...I don't know what I'm going to say.

In the morning Burr and I stand on the step to greet our parents. Strength in numbers, we say. My heart is fluttering wildly. "Steady," says Burr, "steady." If I don't speak, will she?

Father slides out of the passenger seat, shuts the car door, and just as he walks toward us, the children swoop around from the backyard, having heard the car. He looks down at his grandchildren, scoops up the youngest and swings him to his shoulders. There's an outcry from the others, who all want a ride. Father will not be looked at, face to face. He could be anyone's grandfather, some pleasant old gentleman romping with his grandchildren before he sets off on his journey home. Has he erased himself so thoroughly? Or have we done it for him?

Maybe he really doesn't remember.

One last scene. After Father's death, I have a dream and I phone Burr to tell her.

A group of people has gathered at our childhood home. Family, friends, workmates of Mother, even drinking partners of Father. We are there to celebrate though what we're cele-brating, I don't know.

When Burr and I walk through the door, we don't see Father. We begin to look for him upstairs and down. "I'll bet he's in the rat-cellar," says Burr, and we go out and walk around the side of the house. We have to push back the bushes because spiraea has grown over the double trapdoors. We raise the slats and descend the ladder; look at each other and prepare to hold our breath. But here something happens. The earth cellar opens into an amazing network of rooms underground. We understand now that this is where Father lives. He's been bringing down odds and ends, bits and pieces, for years. He's constructed extra rooms, three of them, and these are roofed and tiled, or lined with wood. Old linoleum has been spread across the floor. There is furniture, a second-hand fridge. I think of the hanging socket and wonder if the fridge has been plugged in.

And now we see Father. He's standing in the middle of the first room, an overflowing bottle in one hand. Champagne— something we've never seen him buy or drink. From above, there are noises of celebration. People shouting, congratulating, many voices. Shall we stay down here to celebrate? There is a moment, when we must decide.

I marvel at how much work Father has done to the place. The walls are neat; the ceilings tight. I move into one of the bedrooms and reach out a hand to smooth the spread—an old one, made of ribbed chenille. I give it a shake to show Burr that look, Father has even carried a mattress down here. But there is no mattress. As I lift the spread, I see the decay, the disintegration of all that lies beneath. In that single moment when I lift the spread to give it a shake, it becomes clear that everything has been eaten by insects, is in shreds, or has rotted away.

But his face. I see Father's face. He has turned toward us while champagne flows over his hand and runs down his arm. He's looking at Burr and me and he's about to celebrate and we clearly see the expression in his streaked and watery eyes.

Earthman Pointing

Roseanne is fidgeting at the sink because she has just watched
Jack walk through the patio screen, face first. The screen went
with him, his right arm scrabbling to thrust it away as his left
propelled his body forward. Jack has had too much to drink;
Roseanne has been counting. To be exact, eight beers and now,
a start on the whisky. Jack wipes his chin with the back of his
hand and hums each time he walks through the kitchen—to
let Roseanne think he's sober and in control. But Roseanne has
been married to Jack 36 years and is on to all of his tricks.

Sometimes, Roseanne attempts to look back over her years with Jack, and sees them, not as years wasted but as time put in. Like everyone else she knows, her time so far has been filled in without her lifting a finger to help it. Years gone. Years spent. And she knows why Jack is drinking tonight—it's the Big-Little book, she's pretty certain. She and Tibbs went too far. They got together this afternoon before the others arrived for the Bar-B-Q, they started acting foolish, and they just went too far.

The others, out on the patio, have finished eating. They're pretending they haven't noticed that Jack has just scrunched the armful of screen into a grey ball and dropped it off the side of the deck. The mosquitoes are sure to start invading; Roseanne crosses the room and slides the glass door so it shuts tight, no crack. She goes back to take up position at the sink and listens through the screen of the kitchen window to hear what's being said. Most of it, she's heard before. Still, she listens because she likes to hear how they twist and tangle the old stories to suit themselves.

Out there, in the semi-dark are: her twin sister, Tibbs; Tibbs' husband Spoke who's been skinny as a blade of grass since they were all nineteen; and Arley, the twins' younger brother. Arley is 56 years old. His wife died last year of sugar diabetes, and Roseanne and Tibbs try to include him in their family gatherings so he won't be lonesome.

Marian is there, too, Roseanne's and Jack's daughter. Marian is 33, has never married and lives in her own apartment on the other side of the river. She is editor of a woman's magazine called *Woman Anew*, and says she's always on the lookout for family stories. Roseanne still hasn't read a word of Marian's that has been recognizable or that has meant a thing to her own life. She and Tibbs think Marian is too serious; they'd like her to write something funny, something that shows the family sense of humour. Privately, to Roseanne, Tibbs says that the readers of *Woman Anew* must think Marian comes from a family that's dead-from-the-ass-up. Roseanne can't say much because Marian is her daughter and she doesn't interfere. But Tibbs, the aunt, can get away with interference both moderate and outrageous. She sat Marian down two weeks ago and said, "Now I want you to promise that you'll write one thing that's funny. Just one. A story, or an article for that magazine of yours. Something that will make me laugh, hear?"

Marian's feelings weren't hurt at all.

As for *Woman Anew*, reading it doesn't make Roseanne feel one bit new; she and Tibbs are the kind of women they are, not really old, certainly not new, just sort of stuck between what Marian's magazine says is happening and what their own lives really are.

When no-one else is around, Roseanne and Tibbs have taken to amusing themselves by thinking up catchy titles for stories and articles; so far, anticipating rejection, they haven't shared these with Marian. Some of the titles they contrive are from items they read in supermarket tabloids: "Shrunken Human Head Found in Peanut Shell," or "Newborn Memorizes *War and Peace*." Others, they just dream up, like "The Case of the Rolling Peas." One of their long-standing inventions is "Earthman Pointing," a title that makes them hoot with laughter because in a harmless way, it both mocks and describes Roseanne's husband, Jack. No matter where they are—on holiday, in the backyard for a Bar-B-Q, at someone's wedding, funeral, standing in the street—anywhere there's a group of people, Jack is always pointing. This is something to do with *Life*, Roseanne thinks, or maybe *Destiny*, she isn't sure. For years this ritual of his has irritated her, even though she tells herself that at least he points in an upward, skyward direction; it's not as if he were pointing to a hole in the ground.

As for catchy titles, Roseanne favours, "The Sardine Coffin," having read about designer coffins in Ghana. An old fisherman had told his daughter that when he died, he wanted to be buried in a sardine. His older brother, a farmer, had been laid out in a carved shallot. Roseanne, if she had the choice, would choose a crane for herself. A whooping crane, elegant and nearly extinct. It would have to be carved thick across the middle, so she could fit inside. The fisherman's daughter in Ghana had told reporters that the sardine coffin was to let people know that her father was a proud and successful fisherman. Roseanne wonders what Marian might write in *Woman Anew* about *her* mother, laid out in a whooping crane? Something humorless, no doubt. And what about Jack? What sort of coffin would *he* choose? Probably a long thick arm with a pointing finger.

Right now, on the patio, they're talking about how a giraffe's blood gets pumped up into its head. "Their necks are over eight feet long," Arley says. "Must be a hell of a heart to get the blood all the way up there, to its brain." Then they switch to Tibbs' husband Spoke, who back in high school had been nicknamed *Giraffe*. It's the Thanksgiving story; they're into Memory Lane, now. Roseanne doesn't know how they move from one story to another so quickly. One thing she does realize, is that all of them—herself included—talk about their past as if it had been cut from fresh crisp paper, only yesterday. And they seem locked into a period that stretches from childhood to early marriage and includes only events that can be made to seem hilarious. Nothing recent, nothing grim allowed. This includes the past 25 years.

In the Thanksgiving story, Spoke is standing on a dining-room chair screwing in a new lightbulb or maybe unscrewing an old, moments before fourteen people sit down to dinner. Spoke loses his grip and the bulb explodes on top of the turkey, just taken out of the oven and set at the end of the table for carving.

Every time this story gets told the number of people around the table changes and the person screwing the lightbulb changes. Sometimes it's Roseanne's husband Jack, sometimes it's Arley, sometimes it's even the twins' Daddy, before they all left home and got married. Now, they're saying it's Spoke and maybe they're right, for all that. Spoke, as long and lean at 59 as he was in those early years when he and Tibbs started going out together. (When Tibbs first brought Spoke home, their Daddy took a good look at him standing at the back door and said, "Who let the air out of you?")

What Roseanne remembers is that Thanksgiving dinner was at her house that year and that the turnips, mashed potatoes and gravy had not yet been put out or she'd have had to dump them in the garbage. Cranberries and pickled beets did get dumped, millions of glass fragments glittering across Roseanne's sparkling white table. She and Tibbs ran every dish back to the kitchen sink for a rinse, wiped the cutlery, and stood on the front step with their backs to the storm door shaking out the tablecloth while, inside, the men peeled the skin right off the turkey, gave it a few swipes with a dish towel and served it up anyway. Underneath the skin was another of Roseanne's perfect turkeys. Jack, in a red apron, posed at the end of the table for a photo and pointed to the ceiling with his carving knife and fork.

Roseanne is still listening at the window, all the while keeping an eye on Jack. So far—and for this Roseanne is grateful—Tibbs has held her tongue about Jack's drinking. It's part of being a twin, knowing when to speak your piece. Privately, Tibbs will no doubt invent some theory that will have to do with Jack's sixtieth birthday coming up. She'll say that Jack missed his change-of-life earlier and then she'll tell about Spoke who went through his, right on the stroke of 50. She and Spoke went through their change together, according to Tibbs, and it wasn't all buttercups and roses, but they came out the other side. She told Marian she'd be happy to write a family story about *that*.

Jack wants another whisky; Roseanne can tell by the way he's pacing around the picnic table. He glances toward the window every few minutes, knowing Roseanne is at the sink, but he's unwilling to come in again after walking through the screen. Roseanne pours herself a glass of wine, curses the Big-Little book, wonders if Tibbs needs a refill, and hears Marian's voice. "Come on out, Ma, we're telling stories. Leave the dishes. We'll do them up later."

"I'll go in and drag her away from the sink," Tibbs says. "She's up to her elbows in you-know-who."

Roseanne hears laughter and by the splurt of it knows right away who they're talking about, now. That sort of outburst is always about Harold Beavis, who followed the twins around when they were in senior high. Harold was a dumpling of a man and when he walked, what you saw from behind were the cheeks of his bum sliding, one up, one down, as if the two weren't connected. Roseanne and Tibbs never liked him because crudeness used to come out of his puffy mouth— smutty queries as he followed them through the halls. *What's that warm thing you two hide under your skirts? How about doing triplets, girls?*

Ten years after they all finished school, Harold Beavis drowned in the river that ran through town, just a block from where he lived. His drowning is the reason Tibbs never drinks from the town water supply, even though the drowning was more than 25 years ago. The person Roseanne feels sorry for is Spoke; ever since Harold drowned, Spoke and Tibbs have been hauling water from a natural spring, 33 miles out of town. Once a week they load up the car with plastic jugs and bottles, even in winter when there are treacherous ice slides around the spring. This has become a family joke ("Have you noticed Harold's a little sweeter since spring runoff?" "Is that Harold, again, dripping out of the tap?"). Tibbs has been teased for years but she's made up her mind: not one drop of fat Harold will get inside her, even on her teeth.

Roseanne, believing this to be irrational, understands. Who could know Tibbs better than her own twin? And has Tibbs ever said a word to Roseanne about pork?

On her fortieth birthday, Roseanne started work as part-time cashier at the Auction Barns. More money changed hands on paper at the Barns than she would have thought existed in the whole world. She got used to this, and the men liked her because she was quick and could keep up with rapid-fire transactions. At the Barns, which were on the edge of town near First Bridge, she was known to the men as Rosie. It was Rosie this and Rosie that. She stayed in that job for six years and quit on a Friday morning—the day the late Shank Brady's pigs were auctioned off. One of the men who worked the ring sidled over and said, "You see that big sow over there, Rosie? Whoever eats a piece of bacon out of that hide will be eatin' a piece of Shank Brady." Sure enough, though only a few people knew, the pig had killed Brady, eating the guts right out of him when Brady had fallen into the pen.

Since that very Friday, Roseanne hasn't eaten so much as a slice of ham or bacon, or cooked a roast of pork. She eats beef and a little chicken, now, but every time she passes the meat counter in the A & P she thinks of Shank Brady head first in the pigpen, the old sow chomping on his insides.

Tap water and pork. These are the twins' deprivations.

Roseanne slides back the glass door and lets herself out onto the patio where the others are sitting in a circle, slapping at mosquitoes. Jack sees his chance and shoots past her into the kitchen. Across the darkness, Tibbs raises her eyebrows and she and Roseanne exchange meaningful looks.

Spoke is saying, "Purple martins aren't that easy to attract; I've been trying for years."

"The *Darth Vaders* of the swallow world," says Marian, blackly. "That's what they look like to me."

"Jack knows all about birdhouses," Tibbs says. "He built

two last year. Put them too close together, Roseanne and I kept telling him. One of them blew down in the first windstorm. The other is still attached to the tree."

Roseanne's version of this story begins earlier though it's true that one house did blow down.

Jack built the birdhouses with holes so small, no bird could get in. He set the ladder against the tree and climbed. He checked the measurements and said the holes were exactly right; if he were to make them larger, sparrows would take over. Swallows did try but could get only head and breast in before they struggled and heaved and flapped back out.

After two days of watching unsuccessful entries Roseanne convinced Jack to make one hole larger. Back up the tree he climbed, pointing his file skyward. He rubbed at the wood and came back to the kitchen to stand at the window with Roseanne. Just then, a sparrow flew straight into the hole, plugged it and stuck there. Feet and tail thrashed and flailed as the bird tried to dislodge itself.

Thinking of the bird's head in the dark, thinking of the descending lid of her crane, Roseanne said, "It's terrified, Jack. It's going to have a heart attack."

Out came the ladder again. Jack climbed, cursing all feathered vertebrates, and enclosed the bird in one of his large hands. He tugged it backwards out of the hole. The bird stilled; only its head emerged from Jack's curled fingers. Jack stretched his arm and opened his hand, pointing toward the sky. At first, the bird didn't move; then, it seemed to become an extension of Jack's fingers, and flew off. Roseanne felt the stirring of an old surge of affection for Jack that day, watching the sparrow in his hand, watching him set it free. A few hours later, the swallows returned and built their nest. But before the eggs had a chance to hatch, the house blew down.

Jack must have slipped out the front door and come quietly around the side of the house; Roseanne sees his silhouette near the tree. He's down at the end of the yard, acting like an alien, a stranger lurking at the outer edges of a family gathering.

In the shadows, he raises his glass; for a moment Roseanne expects him to point it skyward as he did the bird. He does not; he downs the contents, probably whisky again, in one gulp. And stays there, by the tree.

She sees now that making fun was the worst offence. She and Tibbs could have made the book and never shown it, and Jack would be none the wiser. It's all so much silliness, she thinks, all his damned waving and pointing and gesticulating. If he's that thin-skinned all of a sudden, maybe he is going through the change.

She wishes she could remember how she and Tibbs got started in the first place. Maybe they were thinking up titles for Marian's sour-grapes magazine. She remembers trying to match catchy titles to photos but she can't remember whose idea the Big-Little was. All she knows is that in the afternoon she and Tibbs were sprawled out on the living-room rug, cutting and pasting, laughing until their cheeks hurt. It had not been difficult to find photos of Jack among the albums and cigar boxes. Jack with a point for every occasion: an arm, an index finger outstretched, a stick, a hoe, a carving knife, a shovel, a baseball bat, a piece of driftwood, a fishing rod— pointing at, but at what? At the end of the driveway? At the hedge, the turkey, the flying saucer, the dunes, the flag, the migrating geese—the beyond?

What she and Tibbs had done in their great flush of laughter and craziness was to cull the photos and paste them on construction paper, each photo having its own page. Jack's point was manoeuvred so that it was always aimed toward the upper right corner. They cut and shaped and produced their own Big-Little book, 22 pages long. They stapled the cover and with felt pens, printed its title: *Earthman Pointing*. And then, shrieking and holding their sides, took it to Jack to show him. The book had enough thickness so that when they thumbed the upper right corner, riffling the pages, the effect was that of Jack in rapid motion, Jack with finger in the air, swinging his implements of destiny.

But Jack had not laughed. Had not thought this funny at all. Something in his face tightened, and while Roseanne did not miss this entirely, she and Tibbs had already gone too far to turn back. They flipped the Big-Little under his nose; their laughter flattened—and died.

Yes, making fun had been the worst offence and she and Tibbs had committed it. No wonder Jack is standing down there in the dark drinking whisky beneath the tree.

Roseanne looks at Tibbs across the picnic table. The story-telling has petered out; moments of silence are gathering before everyone starts picking up to go home. Tibbs looks back at Roseanne and raises her eyebrows, and with this exchange Roseanne is caught off guard. Sometimes, looking at her twin is not unlike searching a mirror for her own like-ness. Tibbs wriggles her eyebrow again, unnoticed by Spoke, by Marian, by Arley. She has a smirk on her face and motions toward Jack who has set down his glass and is pointing up to the black black sky.

Roseanne is angry then: at Tibbs for making fun; at the Big-Little; at herself for taking part; at Jack, who sees something Roseanne does not.

Roseanne finds herself wanting, wanting to see, too.

She peers down along the grass. She cannot see the bird-house, just barely sees the outline of the tree. Darkness has settled. Roseanne no longer knows if Jack is even there.

Sarajevo

During takeoff, Margo called up her angels. Morav, she said to herself. She closed her eyes. Daddy. Aunt Elspeth. Uncle Harry. Jill who died before me and was too young. She forgot Grandmother O'Hare and was reminded later the same night. Grandmother O'Hare walked into her dream and stood with a pinched face, severe, silent because she'd been left off the list.

There was a windstorm in Frankfurt but no flights had been cancelled. Margo felt the wing outside her window tip to the left, as if she'd caught the plane in the act of tumbling over.

Tumble. Drop. She'd gone through this so many times in her mind, for so many years, she knew the sequence.

It had been bad enough getting herself across the Atlantic. An act of faith she did not believe she could raise each time she flew across an ocean. Acts of innocence and faith to believe as the plane drifted away from one continent and entered the abyss over cold bottomless Atlantic, that it could and would reach the opposite shore. Always night flights. Flying out over darkness. Hard cold ocean with all its creatures great and small, lurking below. Never, when she set foot on a plane, did she have a single expectation of arriving at destination. If it happened, it was a gift, a blessing, a miracle.

Between Frankfurt and Zagreb, the Croatian stewardess presented a meal heavy with meat, a layer of cold grease visible. Margo rejected it, turned away, wondering how, why, she had entered this new set of risks and possibilities. War. Warriors. She was married to a warrior who'd been away from home almost a year. That was why she had left Frankfurt in a windstorm, and was headed for Zagreb.

She phoned her friend Marion before leaving.

"Marion? I've got my ticket."

"You're sure you want to do this?"

"Want has nothing to do with it. I *have* to do this. He's out of Bosnia now. He's living in Croatia. But he goes *back in* just about every week. The last time I talked to him a Serb had held a gun to his head."

"What did he do?"

"He said to the Serb's companion—another Serb—'Ask him if it's because he has such poor aim that he has to stand this close to shoot me.'"

"Was Geoff armed?"

"No. He hates wearing a gun. I don't know what he's thinking but he's not afraid. He believes *Right* not *Might* will have its way. He truly believes that. Despite what his eyes are seeing."

"He doesn't think about death the way we do," said Marion.

116

"How is that?"

"I don't know. Fear, I guess."

"He doesn't think about it at all. He says if he were to think about death in the middle of a war, he'd already be dead."

"He's probably right," said Marion.

A week earlier, a UN soldier's face had been carved with a knife, at gunpoint. And snipers, there were always snipers. They picked off whomever they could—their own civilian population, UN peacekeepers, aid workers. In downtown Sarajevo old women out for firewood or water were shot at for target practice. Cowards. Cowardly men hiding behind guns, shooting at their own elderly, their own children. She hated, detested Geoff being there. Last year his arm had been broken when a Croat had tried to kidnap him. Geoff had not been shot, nor had he been kidnapped. But he'd walked away from a cocked machine gun. He believed in his work. He didn't see Muslims, Croats, Serbs. He saw humans needing help. Children—many children. Orphans. Women. Some men. The old. He knew individuals. Friends. Teenagers. Victims. All of them victims of their own war. There were days, nights when she regretted loving him.

Days and nights were all alike in the hotel. They lived in the country, outside Zagreb, a rural stretch of four-lane dusty highway. The hotel had been taken over by the United Nations. From the outside it was baby blue, a long flat building, concrete and glass. She felt like Rapunzel on the second floor, alone all day, Croatian police guarding her from outside. They swaggered into the Bar in the morning where she, the only customer, sipped bitter coffee and kept watch over knives and guns strapped to their waists. The waiters wore blousy shirts and in halting English spoke with her about *gut Geld* in Kingston and in Frankfurt. Every one of them had a brother, uncle or daughter in Canada or Germany. No-one, it seemed, wanted to stay in Croatia.

In the evening, the warriors came back from headquarters, lining up their white vehicles like cardboard jeeps in the parking-lot below. They were from many nations, European and African. Geoff was first to leave in the morning and last to return at night. He flew in and out of Bosnia by helicopter, by small jet, continuing his journeys in open jeeps or armoured personnel carriers for the final leg. One morning a bullet ripped through the cockpit of the plane as the pilot landed. Geoff was sitting behind the navigator. The bullet exited inches from his ear. In their hotel-room, he painted his blood group on the back of his blue helmet. Large permanent felt tip letters so there'd be no mistake.

Some part of him, she knew, had been drawn to the danger. He talked with resignation and inevitability about the violence. He told her of thugs who'd emerged from the deepest crevices of the earth when war began. Territories had been drawn; the slime-balls, as he called them, would stop at nothing to keep their guns, their endless supply of liquor women money drugs. Their power. War would not end, not with signed agreements in Geneva, London, Sarajevo. No, it was already far beyond three political parties lining up continual complaints to make one another look bad. She could not speak to him of home, of their children. She watched, waited, trying to learn what he was dealing with. Sometimes he stayed in Bosnia several days at a time. He left his gun locked in a trunk in their room. His friends were in Sarajevo. He'd left them behind. He could get out. He was alive. Word of the killings always reached him. Another soldier, another interpreter, a driver, horrible intentional murders. He felt each one, shook his head, talked to her as if they were alive. Some, a few, had got out. He'd helped. He received letters at the hotel, passed through many hands, filled with tears, with kisses, with love. When he returned each time from Bosnia, his back was soaked through under the armour he wore. The equipment too heavy to carry. He removed it piece by piece in their room, stacked it in a corner, the blue helmet placed on top with his blood group showing, reminding them of what was necessary, of what might be.

During daylight she walked for hours each day, along open four-lane highway where she would be safe. Past dusty cornfields. Flat plain. Men looked at her with anger, knowing she was a foreigner. She wore dusty old clothes for walking. Found paths through the field gardens, greeted women bent double over small patches of earth. No-one returned her greeting. Never. The women were hostile, suspicious. She returned to the highway, ignored the horns of trucks. She sat at the window and watched the Croatian police below. Wrote long letters to Marion who wrote back to what she called the land of Godforsake. Marion was her thread joining her to Canada, to home.

Geoff brought food to the room. Bottled water. She went into the city and sat in cafés. She walked everywhere. The faces in the city were the same: sullen, silent, grim. Grim seemed to describe everything, everyone.

She had spoken to Geoff by telephone the night he'd moved from Sarajevo to Zagreb. He'd been sitting on the steps of *the Residency*, he said, waiting for his driver to take him to the airport. Branches were snapping off trees above him, in the garden. Bullets.

"Didn't you think to go inside, to wait for the driver?" she said. She'd held her breath in their kitchen, in Canada.

"No." His voice was thin. "The bullets were higher; they were over my head."

The two of them were invited to dinner in the old city, on one of the wooded hills of Zagreb. The general and his entire staff. The French were polite, tugging sideways at their blue berets when they saw her, shaking hands each time they met in the lobby or the Bar. The general jogged each morning accompanied by his four bodyguards, guns strapped to pouches on their backs. The dinner party was pre-arranged; bodyguards had driven to the ancient hill to inspect the premises, several days before. She said to Geoff, "Isn't it rather a giveaway, to let them know we're coming?" But he shook his head, no, no. This was Zagreb, not Sarajevo, after all. Still, precautions had to be taken.

They drove into the wooded area on a Saturday night. When they stepped from the Landrover, she heard Greek music, Theodorakis, from the front of the restaurant, the public part. Their dining-room was behind: a private closed verandah, partially screened, up three wooden steps. Separate entrance. She and Geoff were last to arrive. The party, around a long narrow table, rose to its feet. Only a few had known she was there, living among them at the hotel. The interpreters were there, too, and office clerks, French and Belgian and Canadian officers, bodyguards and drivers. Eighteen at the table. Several languages spoken. Croatian waiters carried in tray after tray of brandy, slivovitz, red wine. Creamy cottage cheese and plates of ham and dry bread. Before the main course.

The general laughed and parried. His eyes dark. All conversation centred around him. He was used to command and control. Expected nothing else, nor did anyone, at the table. She spoke to the UN interpreters, learned their backgrounds, asked questions. Several hours had gone by when she noticed two empty chairs at the far end of the table, to her right. Moments later, the general stood, a small man. The table rose to its feet. Armed bodyguards surrounded him, two white cars with black lettering waited at the screen door. The general slipped into his vehicle, the car roared off into the night. The Landrover followed; more bodyguards. The party was over instantly.

"What," she said to Geoff, "what have we just been a part of?"

The remaining few drifted toward their own white vehicles, parked along the shoulder. A soft fall night. The air was good here, in the woods. "Why were the chairs empty, at the end of the table?" she asked Geoff. "Two of the bodyguards slipped out," he said. "Half-hour earlier than everyone else. They check the general's car, every inch, above and below, with mirrors, for bombs."

She tried to think of home, of her giant shadow legs striding in the sea at sunset, of the undulating lines of migrating cormorants and geese along the shore of Prince Edward Island. If she ever got home she would give thanks for being, for belonging in that wondrous place.

After Samobor, she began to talk to Geoff about home, about their children, family. They drove to Samobor during his first break in more than three months. It was a Sunday, September; he'd not had two hours off since June. He had to return to work later in the afternoon so he stayed in uniform. Samobor was a fifteen-minute drive from the hotel. The front lines had changed since she'd arrived; they were always changing. The southern outskirts of Zagreb had been hit by rockets the week before. She'd been writing to Marion when the windows in her room began to rattle. Shelling went on most of the afternoon and all night. She and Geoff slept to the sounds of guns, not so distant, nine kilometres away. Samobor had been hit. They'd been told it was the most pleasing village in the area: beautiful, ancient, quiet. Narrow streets, woods, castle ruins above the town.

A mistake. There were no signs of shelling but the people were angry. An old man turned and shouted at Geoff. Youths began to circle. They had left their vehicle on the main road, in the centre of town, along a meandering canal.

The people hated the UN. They knew nothing of those who'd been helped, those who'd been saved. Each party angry because the UN would not take its side. So far, Zagreb had stayed out of the physical war. Samobor had never been touched. Until the rockets. She felt something rising inside her, a state of readiness, she was not certain what. She asked Geoff; he felt it too. Hate all around them. Hate and anger that could turn at any moment.

Flick, she thought. Flick, and we're into chaos. They returned to their vehicle, aware of each careful step. They left the village and went back to the dreary hotel. She knew then, that she was going to leave. She'd been in Croatia for months and now she wanted to go home.

A small jet was returning to Canada, a visiting commander. They were offered seats, and they accepted. Geoff would take his leave. He would never be able to use up all that was owed him but he would, at least, take leave. He now had a broken rib. MASH had X-rayed him after a jeep accident during his last trip to the front lines. The rib had snapped in two, would hopefully mend on its own. I have to, she wrote their children, I have to get him out of here, but it may not be in one piece.

The dreams of flying began again. Nightmares lined up, ready to assume their place. Geoff told her she had too much imagination as if it were some extra affliction she carried. It was true that she could imagine anything. At the hotel, the navigator told them they'd fly first to Italy, staying overnight; then, to Iceland, then Halifax. The more luggage they carried, the more often they'd have to stop to refuel. She began to dream about Iceland, about drifting over open water, the engine chugging its last before the plane could reach Newfoundland. They were to depart in two days. She'd never crossed the Atlantic in an eight-seater plane.

They flew to Ancona first, on the coast of Italy, and spent the night. She saw Geoff smile, heard him laugh for the first time in many months. Flowers bloomed in Ancona. Voices lifted in ordinary tones, which she thought of as celebratory. She realized she'd lost the sound of normal conversation. She felt as if she were rejoining life after a long time in a darkened tunnel.

When they left Iceland, last chance to refuel before Canada, her thoughts broke to pieces, chasing one another. She did not want to have to call up her angels. The night before, in Ancona, after a long walk on the beach, a long wonderful meal, she'd dreamed of this tiny plane. Inter-city trains had roared below their hotel, between gardens and beach. Close enough to keep her awake most of the night. She had heard the co-pilot say, before she'd boarded in Italy, "Oh, are the brakes fixed?" and knew it was intended as a joke. She was not able to laugh. They were on the military side of the airport and while waiting to board she had been free to wander through the cluster of canvas tents set up like a small village, boardwalks linking one to another.

Burned and blistered children had been arriving on stretchers, IVs dangling above them. Sarajevo to Ancona. A few getting out. A country here, a country there, accepting them. She'd talked to some of the Canadian soldiers working there. To them, Bosnia was a place of bloody war, unseen, that sent out its children on stretchers, innocent and wounded. That was their portion, their reality. At the end of their working day these Canadian men and women slept in clean hotel beds and drank *cappuccino* and ate good meals. They loaded tons of flour stacked like sandbags, and worked in tents lined with maps and makeshift comforts.

Everyone's reality differed. There was no use breaking anything down to its simplest parts. She'd heard Geoff laugh, the old remembered unrestrained laugh that released the tightened lines of his face. He'd laughed only once, but it was a beginning, after Sarajevo. If death came at you unexpectedly, she thought, okay. But not from guns behind buildings, from snipers high on dope or slivovitz. Murderers who were not even your enemies. Who did not know the expressions your face was capable of, or the shape of your fingers, or the colour of your eyes.

She stepped inside her house. *Her* house during the past year, *their* house now. Left the luggage in the living-room, was not interested in opening suitcases or hanging clothes. She knew

123

there was a bottle of champagne in the refrigerator. Good champagne. Dry, the way she liked it. Geoff walked from room to room, every room upstairs and down, examining, as if he had not believed anything would be here when he returned. He lifted a dish, opened a cupboard door, peered into framed photographs of the children. It was late, they'd been travelling fifteen hours. They drank the champagne and hauled out the sheets and made the bed.

It was then that she began to tell him all that she had imagined before they left and all that she had imagined during flight. The sounds she'd heard, the expressions she'd watched, her head filled with details she'd been afraid, until now, to release. He began to laugh, great shaking laughter. She began to cry. Her sobs defeated him. Then they both laughed and cried together. "Why," he said, "why are you crying like this?"

"Because I've earned the right," she said. "I've earned the right to cry this hard."

Flashcards

When Mariko was a child growing up in Steveston, the schoolyard was divided. I don't know why, she said. I don't know why they built that fence. White children on one side, Japanese on the other.

Inside the school, the classroom was divided, too. That goes back a long way. As far back as the twenties. Maybe before Mariko was born.

MOMMA: *The dolls*

One by one the dolls arrived. All the way from Japan. First, for the births of our sons, two boys, one after another, Tadao and

Hiroshi. Then, for Kimiko, our daughter. Most of the dolls, I put in the glass case but the others were in the *tokonoma*, the special corner. The children didn't play with them but they looked and touched...they knew how special they were.

The dolls were large, brightly coloured, lots of reds and golds. Some were dressed in clothes of an upholstered fabric, others were made of silk. And the folds in the sleeves of the kimonos, if you could have seen them! The boys' dolls were *Samurai* warriors, some with separate horse and leather armour. I don't know now if they were made of wood, or lacquered...but handmade. Real hair, black hair, and fine-featured faces. Special ceremonial dolls arrived for *Boys' Day, Girls' Day*. Relatives sent them, relatives who'd never met the children. The dolls came by boat, wrapped so carefully, shipped in wooden boxes and packed in straw.

Well, rumour was going around...this was after Pearl Harbor, you know...December-January-February. I was pregnant with Fumiko...she was born later, in the camp, in '42. Rumour was spreading up and down the coast that on Vancouver Island and even on the mainland, we were going to lose our homes.

Our house was seven years old...a two-storey wooden house. We built it ourselves and bought new furniture, a new stove. We had room for the three children and for the one coming, too.

She wasn't even 25; a good Japanese girl, not a girl, then. Mariko, married to Shiro, fisherman of Ucluelet; Mariko, mother of sons, mother of one daughter, another on the way. When Shiro came in from the boat he rowed across the inlet and went to the dances with his friends. Danced with the cannery girls. Mariko was a good Japanese girl, a good wife...

I didn't know how I would manage...Tadao not yet six, and then Hiroshi; Kimiko no more than a baby herself. What should we take? What should we leave behind? Some of the

Japanese did not believe the rumours, but I...I believed them. I was afraid.

Shiro said that we would take the new stove. He began to build a crate on the beach in front of the house. If we're headed for the mountains, he said, we have to keep warm. Nobody knew when we might be evacuated, which day. Shiro finished the crate for the stove. Two days later—the knock at the door. It was eight o'clock in the morning. "Two hours," we were told. "Two hours to pack your things. Take only what you can carry."

Think of it.

By ten o'clock I had to have the children fed and dressed in warm clothes. I had to prepare food for the journey. We were living on the Island then, Ucluelet...we hadn't been told how long we would be travelling or where we were going. I had to pack only what we could carry from the house. Two hours.

We already had a wood fire going that morning but Shiro said, no matter what, he was bringing the stove. Later, I was glad. He had to cool it fast, take it apart piece by piece, all the pipes down, too. There were puddles all over the place because the only way to cool the stove was with water. He got the stove into the crate. By then I had the rice balls ready and I'd filled the willow basket: rice-pot, food, bedding, clothes for the children, a few dishes...I left two entire sets of Japanese dishes behind, one a wedding gift from my mother. And the children were frightened...frightened into silence. Sometimes Shiro was impatient with them, and in that two hours, all he had time to do was crate the stove.

We took nothing else.
Family documents
furniture
linens
silver
china
photograph albums

wedding gifts
heirlooms
radio—confiscated by police
camera—confiscated by police
Shiro's boat—taken away.
Everything, everything, left behind.
We never saw the house again.

Later, when the kids drove me to Ucluelet, this was 50 *years* later, you understand, there was no house. I could hardly recognize our bay.

But the dolls. Let me tell you about the dolls. We didn't know the date, but we were certain something terrible was going to happen. The way it turned out, the night we decided what to do with the dolls was twelve hours before we were taken from our homes. Next day, our family was the first group of Japanese to arrive at Hastings Park. I was put in a cattle stall with the children for two months before being sent to the camp. Shiro was taken away, separately, with the men.

There were eight families in our bay in Ucluelet. All of the men were fishermen; each had his own boat. All of the boats had been impounded. Shiro had already turned in our boat at New Westminister and had made his way home with the other men. The men gathered together to make decisions and each came to his wife to say what we must do with the dolls.

You see...it was as if the dolls were the most valuable possession we had. They linked our children to their ancestors, to the old country, even though most of us were second and third generation and had never been to the old country. The dolls had been sent to honour the children. But there was no space in our bundles.

How could we bring dolls in our bundles to the camps!

The eight families in our bay gathered on the beach. Each family carried its dolls and a little *sake*, the rice wine. We heaped the dolls into a pile and poured the *sake* over them. I

128

told the children that they must not cry. Shiro struck a match, and paused...and then...we stood, in silence, watching the dolls turn to flame.

The men decided everything. Outside the houses they gathered in small groups and listened to the rumours. The twisted terrifying rumours that were becoming their lives. Their newspapers...stifled. Letters...intercepted. Community centres...boarded up. Schools, closed. Radios, taken away. Rumour could travel only on the breath, through the air, whispered by the trees, lifted by waves up and down the fearful waters of the coast. Outside the houses, in groups, the men decided. Until the men themselves became their own worst rumours. Rounded up. Given no promises. Taken away.

SHIRO: Nishi-san

The mounties came and told us to turn in our boats. Every Canadian fisherman of Japanese descent. It didn't matter that we had done nothing. It didn't matter what we thought. We were told only this: the boats must be brought to New Westminster.

Mine was one of the larger boats so it was used to tow four others—under escort of the Royal Canadian Navy. The navy men had never worked the fishing-boats so they managed to damage most of the ones they brought in. My friends and I felt like sinking our boats anyway, and we should have, except for the hope that this was temporary, a mistake, a misunderstanding. After all, how could we support our families without our boats? Every year, from January to October, we were at sea...weeks at a time, sometimes months. There were times when the men who worked for me felt like throwing me overboard—I knew that. But I was known as *high-catcher*. My boat had more fish to sell to the collector than any other man on any day. I knew what I was doing; we caught fish. We looked after one another out there.

But if you could have seen the boats at the Annieville

Dyke...ghosts, more than a thousand roped together in a triangle. Wood rubbing wood, windows gaping to a vanishing point across the water.

Sold

sunk

looted

auctioned off...after the Cabinet allowed the insertion of the clause, "without the owners' consent," so the BC politicians could get rid of our property. Trying to ensure that we'd never go back, that there'd be nothing to go back to.

They got rid of Nishi-san, all right. An old man, a friend of my father. Others his age, they'd already stopped fishing. We all looked out for Nishi-san, you know, on the water. Kept him in sight. But the day the boats were seized, his boat drifted and got into US waters. We couldn't get to him; we had to follow orders, had to tow the boats to the Annieville Dyke. I kept telling the police: I have to go after Nishi-san, I have to help him. I know something's wrong or he wouldn't be drifting like that.

I saw the cabin of his boat when it was brought in. Blood spattered...floor, walls, even on the ceiling. His throat had been cut, a big hole in his throat. We went to visit him in hospital but he died there.

They got him all right. He wasn't able to say who had done it, who had cut the hole in his throat, but they got him, old Nishi-san, an old man who had never hurt anyone. He was just out there trying to catch fish for a living, trying to stay alive.

One day Mariko went out on the boat. Only once. We'll go for the day, he said. I'll get you home before nightfall. So she asked her sister to stay with the children and she said to him, I'll go.

Drop your line, Shiro told her. Drop your line. Let it out and you'll catch a big fish.

Was he making fun?

This was before he put out his own wide nets; first, he wanted her to catch a big fish. But as soon as she let out the line, the hook snagged and almost stopped the boat. He came back and stood beside her; took the line and pulled, impatient, because she'd tangled. You only have 60 feet of line, he said; now he was laughing...we're in 500 feet of water. You must have caught one of those big creatures that live down there under the waves. They're covered with hair and have two hind legs.

She didn't think that was funny; she knew about unspeakables lurking at the bottom of the sea.

Shiro manoeuvred the boat in a circle and yanked the line, hard. When he yanked she saw the set of his face and he said, That's no fish. Up came the hook just as he spoke, as if it had been pushed fast through the waves.

What she saw first was flesh, gobbed to the hook, two inches thick. Skin. What looked like brain. He threw it back so quickly there was no time to think about it, or examine.

Body, she said through her teeth. She hated recalling it later. Body, she said, and she never went out on the boat again.

SHIRO: Friend

My closest friend Jimmy was taken directly to a detention centre in Vancouver. After that he was sent by train to Ontario to a prisoner-of-war camp. At the time we didn't know where he was going or why. We still don't know why. Some of the men were singled out like that, though Jimmy was a fisherman like the rest of us.

He came to say goodbye while we were packing. I was nailing the crate that held the hot stove. Mariko was getting the children ready, trying to pack the bundles. I'd never seen Jimmy dressed like that—I was used to seeing him on his boat. He had on his good blue suit, a long winter coat, a fedora. He looked like an imposter in Jimmy's good clothes. He walked into the kitchen, didn't take off his shoes...the only time anyone ever walked into the kitchen with shoes on but what did it matter, the floor covered with soot. He walked in and looked at me. I was standing beside the crate with the hammer in my hand. We'd been friends since we were boys.

We looked at each other, there was so much to say. We said nothing. There weren't enough words in any language to say what we had to say.

MOMMA: *Doorways*

I stood in the doorway of the livestock building at Hastings Park and saw the open stalls. Shiro wasn't with me, he'd been herded somewhere else, with the men. I placed my hand over the baby inside me. I thought I would vomit from the smell. I couldn't believe we were expected to live there. Like cattle. In the animal-urine stench. We arrived after such a long day...so tired...even the children loaded with bundles. First, by boat from Ucluelet to Port Alberni. Then, by train to Nanaimo; ferry to Vancouver; and brought, under guard, to Hastings Park.

Hers were the first eyes to see. Hers, the first nose to smell. Manure. Urine. Lime. Dust. Toilets, a sheet metal trough. No partitions, no seats until later, when the women clamoured.

Hers, were the first eyes to see. Then, through the doorway, hundreds, thousands of eyes pressed forward from behind. Thousands of eyes came after her, staring. Thousands of eyes, prying.

She closed her face so others would not be witness to her private shame.

Right away, I started to scrub. There were maggots; it was impossible to get rid of them. I asked for disinfectant but still the maggots were there. Even on the pallets where we slept on straw and in the manure under the boards of the stalls. I wrapped coats around the children to keep out the damp and the cold. But the maggots were everywhere. I tacked a bedspread around the bunk assigned to me and the children. There was no place to take off our clothes; there was no privacy with families three feet away on every side. Between our stall and the next there were no doors. I hung the bedspread, and

132

climbed up onto the straw tick when I wanted to undress the children or change my clothes.

Day and night, water flowed through the troughs circling the aisles of concrete where thousands of women and children like us were held, under guard. If a woman rinsed clothing in a stall farther up the aisle, soapsuds drifted past and her bubbles stuck to our planks of wood. Through another doorway, there were ten showers...for fifteen hundred women. And more maggots. Once a week we dragged our straw ticks outside the building so the stuffing could be removed and new straw put in...because of the damp and the mould.

Our meals were taken in a separate part of the building, the poultry section, where long wooden tables were set up for more than a thousand Japanese. We ate in that lime and poultry smell. Because I had to feed the children, and help them, many times when I went to get my own meal, later, there was no food left. And always, a mountie stood guard, watching, watching, as we ate.

My younger brother was put to work in the kitchen. Whenever he could, he came to the doorway—men were not permitted in the same building as women and children—and the guard let him hand in cookies for the little ones. Between lunch and dinner sometimes he had extra time, so he baked cookies and the guard let him hand them in. All this time, more and more Japanese were coming through the doors, and the first groups were beginning to go away.

Every day, now, every day a small crowd stands by the tracks. Tracks that lead away from what they know, tracks that lead away from those they love. Displaced Canadians. Families divided. Some trains carry the young men to Angler, Petawawa, Schreiber, where they must wear targets on their backs. Others go to interior road camps. The older generation, the Issei, go with the Nisei to Greenwood, Kaslo, Slocan, Tashme...

The children by these tracks do not play. They hold tight to their bundles and move close to Momma as the train thunders in. Pacific

Great Eastern, clouds of cinder dust. Don't look back, Momma tells them. Your father will find us. He is helping the old people. He is looking after the sacks of sugar and the rice. He has to be sure the crate that holds the stove is loaded on the train. Lift your feet high, children, lift your feet high to reach the step. She turns her head away as the mountie lifts the children, as he stands them in the doorway of the coach.

The children rub their hands against the bristles of the seats. Momma looks out the window. Doesn't seem to hear, now. Hears nothing but the beating heart of the unborn. The world closing down. Drawing in. Shrinking as it chokes. The train jerks and halts, jerks again. The mountie, the conductor, walk the long corridor and remove every white linen rectangle that is buttoned to the headrests. No Japanese head will rest against these. The odours of the train rise and swell: varnish, from the wood panelling; urine; spittoons outside the washrooms where the old men stand and argue and talk. Shiro takes his place across from Mariko and beside the children. The station disappears beyond thick distorted glass. Momma closes her eyes. Thank God, she whispers. Thank God the family is together.

After two months in the cattle stalls we were taken to Squamish and boarded a train for Lillooet. By then Shiro was allowed to come with us. The people of Lillooet didn't want us, so we had to stay on the train all day while they decided what to do with us—the mounties, the government people, the people of the town. Eventually, we were allowed to get off the train but for the next three weeks we lived in a tent. Never again have I felt the cold the way I did in that tent across the river from Lillooet. The children were bundled and wrapped and blanketed. I did everything I could to keep moving, to be warm...I was in the fifth month, then, of my pregnancy. Outside the tent, Shiro put the stove together so we were able to cook and heat water and bathe the children. We chipped in with another family and bought a big galvanized tub and once we had the tub the children were able to have a bath every night—even though we lived in the tent. We knew what had to be done. We helped one another. We did what we had to do.

We were not allowed in the town, so we built our shacks in a field four miles away, across the Fraser. Sixty-three shacks for one hundred and three families. We had to pay for our drinking water, which was brought in by truck. Many of the children had diarrhea after drinking this water and in the early days some of our old people died of dysentery. In a camp north of us, some died of typhoid. Later, an old flume was repaired and water was diverted from mountain streams for bathing and irrigation.

That's where we lived. Until 1947 when we moved to Greenwood. Five years. We paid for our own internment. We had to promise the government that we could support ourselves, so Shiro cashed in our only insurance policy to pay for the shack. He and my brother did the construction themselves.

There was no door for our shack until doors for the entire camp were ordered from Vancouver and sent, weeks later. For a long time, we lived in one room until Shiro was able to put up a partition. That was our living and sleeping space for five people.

The first thing I did when we moved out of the tent and into the shack was to tack a blanket across the open doorway. The open doorway bothered me because of the wild horses. Wild horses roamed the fields on the side of the mountain in the early morning and in the evening. Often, they galloped around the shacks. One night I heard a big noise, like an explosion, a big snorting sound, and I woke up and there was a horse's head beside me. The horse had pushed through the blanket, into our shack. Shiro didn't wake. The children didn't wake, even with all the noise. But my heart pounded for the rest of the night. A horse's head, pushed right in through the doorway!

KIMIKO: Stories

Everyone we knew owned stories. For years our family was piecing together our own, our life stories—of Ucluelet and

Vancouver, of the separation, of the journeys, stories of the camps.

Our Grandma, the one we called *Vancouver Baachan*, owned a grocery store on Powell Street. She was sent to Lemon Creek three months after we were sent to Lillooet. She didn't have to move into the stalls at Hastings Park because she lived right in Vancouver but she had to obey the curfew. Her story was the story of the two-dresser set and she told it over and over, even when she was an old old woman.

She and my grandfather had moved to Vancouver and bought the store after he retired from fishing. There was a woodstove in one corner, and a couple of long benches. They lived in two rooms at the back of the store. The old men in the community came by in the morning to sit around and argue and gossip. After Pearl Harbor they still came, only this time, in confusion. Who had disappeared since the day before? Was there any news? What was happening?

The police strolled by in pairs; they'd get past the store and then turn around suddenly and charge in as if they expected to uncover some unthinkable operation. The old men blinked and became silent and went back to their homes. One by one these old men were taken away, even our grandfather, our *Jichan*. After that it was the wives who came to talk and sew and visit *Vancouver Baachan*. Sometimes one of the women would have a letter to share and some news about where one of the husbands had been taken. The police kept strolling by in pairs and charging in but now they found only the women, sewing. The women, too, became silent until the police went away.

Vancouver Baachan knew she'd have to sell off her belongings and of course she lost the store, but what she was most proud of was her two-dresser set. Polished mahogany. "A two-dresser set," she told us, many times. "In those days, that was something. After my children were grown I saved every penny. Who ever thought I'd live to own a two-dresser set."

136

She was alone in the store the day the pickup arrived to carry it away. She was paid $6—the best price she could get. She stood at the window and watched two men load it. She watched it drive away. The truck turned the corner and long after it was gone she stared out the window. She could not make herself move. When she told us this story her eyes were always following the two-dresser set on the back of that pickup, driving away from her store.

TADAO: Icicle Hill

I'll tell you the story I know about the camp. Hauling water, that's what I know. Father built a yoke to place across my shoulders and from the yoke, a bucket was suspended on each side. I had to go across the road and down a hill to get to the water tanks and the path was steep. My shoulders remember that climb. My back remembers that climb. In the winter, most of the time the path was a slide of ice. I called it icicle hill. The old people in the camp couldn't carry their own water so I brought it up for them. That was my job from the time I was six. Hauling water. I must have done other things, too, but what I remember is this: hauling water up that goddamned icicle hill.

MOMMA: The baby

Fumiko was born, and when the afterbirth came I saw the midwife shake her head. I began to bleed...and then the bleeding turned to haemorrhage...and after that I lost a lot of blood, very much blood, and I lay there on my back, and told Shiro I knew I was going. I could feel myself slipping away.

Shiro sent a message across the river to the doctor...we were not allowed in Lillooet without a permit...and after many hours, a veterinarian came to the camp and gave me an injection. I guess that's what stopped the bleeding. I was weak for a long time because I had lost so much blood...I was weak for more than a year.

Fumiko died after three days though to me she had looked beautiful and strong. But I remembered the midwife's face when she had looked at the afterbirth.

All those months, Fumiko had survived inside me: through the evacuation from Ucluelet, and on the ferries, and in the cattle stalls, and on the trains, and in the cold tent on the side of the mountain. But when she was born, she lived for only three days.

How could she love a child that much? A child that came from herself, wrenched and torn as she was. The midwife said to Shiro, Your wife must not be pregnant again. She said this sharply, said things to Shiro that Mariko herself had never dared. And who would look after the children, if Mariko were to die?

TADAO: Fumiko's bones

After our baby sister died she was burned in the woods on the side of the mountain, in a clearing where cremations took place. Hiroshi and I were each given a pair of special chopsticks and Father told us what we had to do. From the ashes, we were to pick up any tiny bones that remained. Momma gave us one of those round baking powder tins, an empty one, and we had to put the bones in this, one by one, with the chopsticks. Father crouched down and looked at us, straight into our faces, and said we were not to drop a single bone...for Fumiko, we must not. We must not let Fumiko's bones fall back to earth.

I was afraid because of Father's voice but Hiroshi and I, we picked every tiny bone from the smoldering ashes. Momma kept them for many years in that same baking powder tin, long after the war. Years after Fumiko's death, Momma took the bones to a cemetery, far far away from that place.

Oh, the bones rattled in that tin. When they packed up their bundles. When they moved, again and again. Rattled from one shack to another through the mountains, and rattled behind Shiro to the lumber mills, and in flea-infested bunkhouses, and on the running boards of trucks, and south to the farms in the valley. Rattled until the family found a place to halt. Rattled until the bones were shaken out of that tin and planted in the earth. Only then did those bones become SILENT.

SHIRO: New Year

Our first New Year, *Shogatsu*, we didn't have much but I had built a table and long benches and we hung coal-oil lanterns from the ceiling. Early New Year's Eve the children ran out to the bathhouse and scrubbed extra hard, because they remembered their *Vancouver Baachan* telling them that anyone who forgot to bathe before *Shogatsu* would turn into an owl.

When the children were in bed Mariko made *sushi* of egg and rice. For outer wrappings she used cabbage leaves we'd stored in the fall. These were salted and folded and packed in a jar, and rinsed with water as we needed them. When a leaf tore during the *sushi* making, Mariko patched it with a piece from another cabbage leaf.

In the morning, the children were dressed in the best clothes they had, Tadao and Hiroshi each added one of my old bow ties...Mariko made a ribbon for Kimiko's hair. A chicken was cooked, the gramaphone borrowed from house to house, and families visited back and forth all that day and the next day, too.

I thought of our parents, our relatives, in camps like ours and in road camps and in ghost towns throughout BC. I thought of Jimmy. I wondered if he had anything to celebrate. It was years before I saw friends and relatives again. I knew though, I somehow knew that they were thinking of us. The men in our camp were helpless. Alone or together, we were helpless. We did not speak of this because we could not afford to allow the rage. If rage were allowed, it would also consume. We visited our neighbours and ate the *sushi* and the children

139

celebrated. Before we knew it *Shogatsu* was over, and each day that followed was like any other day.

HIROSHI: *Wild horse*

We'd been in the camp only a little while when I made up my mind to catch a wild horse. From the first day I saw them, I loved the horses.

I didn't tell anyone in the family because I was sure they'd say I was too small, too young, too short, to catch a wild horse. I used to watch the Indians who lived nearby. They could ride, and they never used saddles. They seemed to be able to make the horses do whatever they wanted them to do.

So I found myself a 10-inch spike and a length of rope, and I tied the rope to one end of the spike. I believed that if I could figure how to get the rope attached to the other end, the sharp end, and make it stay without slipping off, then I'd get my homemade bit on a horse. If I could get the bit in its mouth the way the Indians did, I could tame it.

I kept a second piece of rope handy so I could use this one as a rein. But whenever I saw the wild horses, I'd have forgotten the bit and the rein at home. I slept with the spike under my pillow and sometimes I'd forget, and leave it there. Even when I had it with me, I couldn't get close enough. I'd go near the horses, they'd skitter to the right; I'd try again, they'd skitter to the left. The horses always got away.

I kept my homemade bit and rope all the years we were in Lillooet. Never once did I stop believing I'd tame a wild horse. All I needed to do was figure how to keep the rope attached to the sharp end of the spike.

Seasons passed one into the other. The wood, always piled high. When the energy of the camp was not put into fields and gardens, it was put into finding wood, chopping wood, clearing deadwood, stacking wet wood, storing dry wood. Having enough wood for next winter and the winter after that.

KIMIKO: *Ji*

The old man we called Ji lived next to us in a shack, with his daughter and his daughter's family. Ji was like a Grampa to us though we weren't related. Ji worked in the garden all summer, and did outdoor carpentry in the spring and fall. His tough old hands were creased with rivulets of cracked dry skin.

In the evenings, he'd come over and sit on a bench outside and he'd tell us his stories. All during the telling, he'd be sewing up the cracks in his fingers with a needle and black thread. Each time he finished a stitch we'd hear a sharp intake of breath; he'd lower his hand to his side and shake it out in pain. I hardly remember a story old Ji told but I can see him now, stitching up the cracks in his own fingers.

HIROSHI: *Bath*

Ji made us a wooden sink though we had no running water. He made it from cedar and it was smooth and had beautiful joints. Ji was the maker of beautiful sinks.

He built our family bath, too. It was separate from the shack, raised in an enclosed shelter. It was made of wood, with a galvanized metal floor and a wooden platform across the bottom to keep us from getting burned. A log fire was kept going in a chamber below the tub. Sometimes we collected rain water, letting it drain through a pipe directly into the bath. Most of the time, we hauled our water from the Fraser.

A pump-house was set up and once a week water was pumped up to fill huge wooden tanks on a hill below the road. Community tanks. As each tank was filled, it was covered over. There were holes in the side of each tank and these were stopped by wooden plugs. As the water level went down, we pulled out a plug lower than the water line so we could fill our buckets.

Every night, all the kids had a bath, and after we were finished, our parents did too. Scrubbing with soap and rins-

ing, and then climbing in for a hot soak in the tub Ji had built
for us. Even in winter, every night, a long hot soak in the tub.

*In rented fields they harvested tomato and corn, carrot and cabbage,
melon, potato and squash. Picked the wild strawberry and Mariko
made jam. Prepared dandelion greens with sugar and* goma *and*
shoyu.

*The men set up an irrigation system to water the fields: long wooden
pipes with homemade wire filters. Cold clear water rushed down from
the mountain currents, rushed from the damned streams into holding
tanks and out the pipes again. Every once in a while someone hauled
out a fat rainbow trout, caught in the pipes, caught between filters. A
rainbow trout, ten inches long, coming down the pipes for dinner.*

KIMIKO: Candy

Ji had a huge copper kettle that he lent to everyone in the
camp anytime it was needed. When we borrowed the kettle it
was for making candy.

First, Momma cooked the syrup until it was very hot.
When it began to thicken, the candy was turned out onto a
board so we could start working it. We made green and red
candy, cinnamon candy and candy with white streaks.

Father had nailed a long spike at an angle into the wall and
he threw the mass of candy across this spike, stretching and
stretching and pulling. He added twists and reverse twists
and stretched and pulled some more; then he cut it into pieces
with sharp scissors. He handed it down to us and we sprinkled
it with powdered sugar.

After the kettle was returned to Ji, Hiroshi and I went back
inside. We pushed a chair under the spike and knocked off the
hardened bits of candy still stuck there. When where was
nothing more to knock off, the two of us stood on the chair and
licked the spike clean.

TADAO: *Kites*

Spring was our time for making kites. We looked for tissue paper, something soft and smooth. If we couldn't find that, Father flattened brown paper bags. We scrounged for string; black ink to draw characters on the finished kite; bones of bamboo. Ji saved bamboo for us from the hoops of old pickle barrels because it split easily into fine strips and was flexible. Ji could tell which pieces had the greatest strength. Father used fishing knots to lash the bamboo together, and for the bridle, fishing line. So much fishing line, not in use.

My job was to cut tiny band-aid strips of paper and fasten them along the skeleton and the edges to hold the larger paper in place. For paste we used leftover rice—sticky, leftover rice. Two grains of rice squished with a thumb and left to dry overnight made perfect paste.

If the kite didn't fly well, Father made fine adjustments to the bridle. He seemed to know just what to do. He knew about placing the bamboo upside down from the way it grows. And he knew about wind that brushed the cheeks of children and wind that puffed down the slopes of the hills.

HIROSHI: *Sold*

Father received word that our house in Ucluelet had been sold. House and contents, sold. Boat was gone, already auctioned off.

The day the letter came Father folded it in half and slowly, deliberately, tore it into strips. He lifted the axe from the nails where it hung on the wall and he went outside. Momma said we had to stay in and she closed the door of the shack.

Father began to chop. He quartered pieces of log and chopped those into kindling, he threw the wood behind him as he chopped. He chopped the rest of the day and refused to come in when Momma called him for supper. He lit a coal-oil lantern and we heard him chopping hour after hour into the night. None of the neighbours came near.

When finally he came into the shack he dropped into bed and slept until noon the next day. When he woke, he spoke to us in Japanese. Father never again spoke the language of our country. After the house was sold, Father never spoke English again.

MOMMA: *Celebration*

We did not sit around feeling sorry for ourselves, there was too much to do—no running water, no electricity, no washing machine, all the gardening, the field work, the cooking and storing and preserving. Then, there were births, marriages, funerals. But several times a year, we paused. The entire community paused.

The men had built a one-room schoolhouse and during late summer and early fall, began to prepare for the play that they would perform there, in November. Every spare moment went to constructing sets and painting backdrops. A new play had to be written each year and the actors had to learn their parts after the harvest. The men played the women's roles, as well.

Among the internees at the camp we had two carpenters, an artist and a man who was good at writing scripts. They took charge, and helped direct the others.

The children fell silent; the storyteller stepped forward with an air of magnificence, settled himself on a stool at the edge of the lantern-lit stage. Two smooth blocks clapped together in a sharpness of sound, an unseen hand set the gramaphone turning, unrecognized fathers took their places on stage. No child saw the rough platform resting low on sawhorses; no child saw fisherman, farmer, millworker. Instead— imposing figures, a whirl of long dark robe, makeup and mask, water- colours lifting and fluttering before their eyes. How they laughed, how they laughed, how their hands flew to their mouths; how they protested and called for more as the curtains were closed. But the actors had run out of script, the jokes had been spent, the evening had come to an end.

MOMMA: Sake

After the play, Shiro and the other men got into the *sake*. Liquor was not permitted in the camp so the men always made their own. Dandelion *sake* and potato *sake*. For weeks it had been brewing and fermenting in brown crocks, with lemons and oranges and sugar.

The men stayed behind at the schoolhouse, sprawled on the stage, half in and half out of costume. We women left them there, and slowly walked home with the children. Much later, when Shiro came stumbling in, I moved to the edge of the bed and bent up my knees, and pretended I was in a deep sleep.

Still the men gathered. Talked. Talked some more. Gathered under the whisper of lodgepole pines and beside woodpiles stacked for winter, and on the edge of cabbage patches and along the dirt road. Talked before the sun came up over the mountain and after the day's work was done. Each day when the men and women came home from the gardens and fields the women went inside to prepare the evening meal but the men stayed out there, talking. Talk victory. Talk defeat. Talk atrocity. Talk bomb. Hiroshima, Nagasaki. Talk loyalty. Talk signing papers, talk government trying to force them to go to Japan.

KIMIKO: Surrender

2 September, 1945: Momma was working in the fields with Father and the boys when the cars came from Lillooet, across the river. I saw our neighbours running toward their houses and I was frightened because I was alone. I ran inside our shack and pulled the curtains tight so it would be dark inside. So it would look as if no-one was there. I kneeled on the floor by the window and watched through a tiny crack. Our whole camp, within minutes, seemed to be deserted but we were there, hiding inside.

The drivers were white people from the town; they blasted horns and drove round and round the camp, back and forth on the main road and between the shacks, honking and shouting.

They did this for about twenty minutes but no-one came out of the shacks. They seemed to tire, suddenly, of roaring through a camp that was silent, so they turned and went honking back toward town.

We knew Japan had surrendered. We were glad, too. There we were, hiding behind the walls because Canada, our country, was no longer at war.

No-one wanted the Japanese living near them. Not during the war, not after the war. We—will—live—through—this, Mariko said. The children must survive. Someday, their lives will be better than this. Shikata ga nai, It can't be helped, Shikata ga nai. There are times when everyone would like to flee from pain. At these times we must find other reasons for living. First, we keep the family together. Then, we find other reasons for living.

HIROSHI: Naming

In '47 our family finally moved away from Lillooet to Greenwood, another camp. From there, like drifters, we moved to Westbank in the Okanagan. That was where we stayed but in Westbank we moved five times in the first three years. One winter, we lived in a chicken coop. The following spring, we moved twice in the same day.

I had started Japanese school in the camps but in Westbank I was finally permitted to go to English school. After the war there were few Japanese there—none in my class. On my first day in Grade 3, the teacher, Miss Paxton, told each of us to stand beside our desk and say our name. When it was my turn I stood and said, "My name is Hiroshi," and I sat down.

"What kind of name is that?" she said. "Stand up and say it again."

I said, "Hiroshi. It's my name." This time she told me to go to the front of the room and print it on the blackboard.

"Isn't that a silly name," she said to the class. "We've never heard of a name like Hiroshi."

The children all laughed, and then Miss Paxton said it was

146

not possible to remember such a silly name. She drew a thick chalk X through Hiroshi and printed beside it, *Henry*.

"This is your new name," she said. "If you're going to come to an English school, you're going to have an English name."

So when I went home from school that first day, I told Momma, "The teacher said I have to change my name to Henry."

After changing my name to Henry, on the second day of school, Miss Paxton said, "Stand up, Henry, and tell us the names of your parents."

So I stood beside my desk, and putting the last name first as I had been taught by my parents, I said, "Higashi, Shiro and Mariko," and everyone just roared, everyone in the whole class.

No-one else in the room was asked to do this.

Every day for the rest of the week, Miss Paxton told me to stand up and say the names of my parents aloud, so the class could start off the day with a good laugh. Miss Paxton was my *sensei*, my teacher, and I did what she told me to do.

She was not able to make me cry.

That was my first week of school in Grade 3.

TADAO: Cadets

I was too small for a uniform when I joined so I had to wait until the following year. I guess they didn't make uniforms that small. I'd been in Army Cadets since I was thirteen. Anyway, I got my uniform in February and I showed up every training night, once a week and every second weekend. Mr. Kearns, a World War II veteran, also a history teacher at the high school, was the commander of our Cadet Corps in Westbank and Peachland. I was the only Japanese boy in Cadets.

In April the list was posted for summer camp, always held in Vernon. I wanted to take the Infantry Signallers' Course, six weeks long. I knew I was in the top ten percent as far as performance; it was mainly a matter of getting permission from my parents. They needed me at home to contribute to the family income by working on the orchards and farms in the valley. I told Mr. Kearns I'd like to go to camp. I guess I should've thought more about the look on his face, at the time. He said I couldn't go for the full course; maybe for two weeks, instead, to qualify. I reminded him that I'd fulfilled all of the prerequisites and then he said there was no vacancy, maybe he could get me there for two weeks.

After a few more weeks the boys in our Corps were given instructions and a list of equipment to bring. I was not given the list. I had permission from my parents but my name wasn't called the night the bus tickets to Vernon were given out.

I went to Mr. Kearns and asked why my name wasn't called. He mumbled something about me going for two weeks and then he was called away and too busy to see me. I tried to see him at school but he was always busy. I wasn't sure what the preparation was or what I was supposed to bring. At the end of the school year I still had no ticket but I knew the date and time the other boys would be leaving. I had one dollar and fifty cents, not enough for a ticket, so I decided to hitchhike. I couldn't ask my parents for money and I didn't tell them that I had no bus ticket.

The cadets left by bus early Sunday. I went out to the gravel road and began to hitchhike but no-one wanted to pick me up, even though I was wearing my new uniform. I carried an old duffel bag with socks, shoe-polishing kit, shirts, things I thought I'd need. I walked a long way and a couple of hours after I started out two women picked me up—white women about the same age as my mother. As soon as I got in the car they told me I had to pay gas money. I'd never hitchhiked before so I thought that's what you were supposed to do. They asked how much I had and I told them a dollar fifty. That's what it costs for gas, they said, so I gave them the money. With all the waiting and walking and finally getting the drive, it took more than four hours to get to Vernon.

I showed up in the afternoon, hours after the boys from

other districts had checked in. A militia corporal and a sergeant from the regular force were on duty in the Orderly Room, and they looked astonished when I walked in off the road. They kept checking the lists—there were over a thousand cadets from BC and Alberta—but my name wasn't on them. The corporal was nice to me, though. He said, "It's all right, we'll look after you, I'm sure we can find a place." I gave them Mr. Kearns' name and said I was from Westbank and that I'd been told I could come to camp for two weeks. They seemed to be scratching their heads over that.

The corporal took me to the Quartermaster so I could draw my barrack box, my bedding and helmet and summer uniform. He led me to the Signals Wing and another corporal, who lived in the building, took over from there. This man was surprised to get an extra cadet but said he had a bunk free. By this time I was pretty scared because I didn't know what to do; the other boys had already been through and had been shown the drill. The corporal taught me how to make my bed, how to look after my uniform—all the things I'd missed in that one afternoon. It was time for dinner and I was wearing the wrong uniform, my winter one, but he said, Don't worry, you can get that sorted out tomorrow, and he showed me where I should go to eat.

Well about four days later, I was being marched along with my platoon on the way to class and I saw Mr. Kearns, who was visiting camp for the day. First chance he had during a break between classes, he came over and said, What are you doing here?

I reminded him that he'd promised I could come for two weeks, that I'd thought something was wrong when I hadn't been issued a ticket, so I hitchhiked. He looked pretty surprised but there was nothing he could do now that I was already there.

Toward the end of my second week, I began to get worried. I knew I'd have to leave, that all the other boys were staying. I was enjoying the course and doing well in the testing. We were just getting into interesting work.

I went to the corporal in charge and asked if I might be allowed to stay. He said he'd never heard of anyone *leaving* after two weeks. Anyone who was there, was there for the whole course. Well, my request went all the way up the chain to the officer. The lieutenant came to see me and said, Look, you're here to stay—do you understand? Six weeks. There's not even a chance that you'll be sent home.

Our first weekend pass I was off from noon Saturday until 10 p.m. Sunday. I hitchhiked back to Westbank and told my parents I had permission to stay at camp until the end of the course. Not only that but I was able to show them $5—my first pay. At the end of the summer, my final pay would be $80, which I'd be able to turn over to them.

While I was home, Father cut my hair—at camp they were always after us to get a haircut. Father had three pair of barber's clippers so I borrowed one and started giving haircuts myself when I got back to camp. There was always a lineup for the regular barber and the boys were usually in a hurry. I charged 25 cents a cut and made about eight dollars a week. Word soon spread around camp that the Japanese kid in Sigs. was cutting hair for a quarter. I made quite a bit of extra money after that. Next time I had a weekend pass, I'd earned enough money to go home by bus. At the end of the summer, the camp adjutant made sure I had a ticket for the trip home. Later, other summers, I became Captain of the Guards and won the trophy for the top cadet in my Corps, two years in a row. Mr. Kearns left local cadets, and we got a new commander.

But Mr. Kearns was my history teacher the following year in Grade 9. One day in class he started teaching the Russo-Japanese war. He taught it as the *Jappo-Russian War*. I put up my hand and said, "Sir, the book says Russo-Japanese War." He started yelling, "It's not. It's NOT. It's the *JAPPO* - Russian War.*" He gave me a detention for that. Everyone in the class seemed ashamed; they kept their heads down but no-one spoke out to back me up, even though every one of us could read perfectly well: *Russo-Japanese War, 1904-1905.*

HENRY: Expression

When we were growing up, an expression in our community went like this:

'If you're good-looking, you're white
If you're ugly, you're Chinese'

We couldn't imagine looking like ourselves...looking Japanese.

MOMMA: Fear

Do you know what I'm afraid of...what I fear the most? After 50 years—I mean, it's been 50 years—after all this time...documents have been released, albums have surfaced, photos taken by police, boxes of papers purchased by archives, books have been written...

Every once in a while, I lift one of these books from the shelf and I open it and look at the faces on the pages. Women's faces—mothers, sisters, daughters. Men's faces, children's, the faces of old people, the *Baachans,* the *Jichans* who were part of our lives. An entire community, 22,000 faces, taken by surprise. As boats were confiscated, as old men stood in line to be stripped of their rights, as old women sat on their bundles, as farms were sold, eldest sons taken away, as faces pressed against the glass of departing trains, as men waved helplessly their day-passes and enemy alien cards. We did not even know who held the cameras that captured us.

What I fear is that, one day, I will turn a page in one of these books and there I'll be, *my* face frozen in impotence and fear. Frozen, turned back, my own face bearing witness to my own shame.

This is what I'm afraid my eyes will see.